# ARTIFICIAL DETECTIVE

by

Dave Terruso

This is a work of fiction. Any resemblance to persons living or dead is purely coincidental.

**Artificial Detective**



Cover art and design by John Lutheran.

ISBN: 978-1-950670-20-8

For Mike Brooks: Watch This.

# 1

"Twenty-four minutes." Detective Leonard Marsden stands beside me, smirking, his right hand resting on my shoulder; he has to stand on his tippy toes to comfortably reach it. "That's how long it took Coba to solve this case that had been considered closed for four years."

Two other detectives, the Atlantic City chief of police, and four patrol officers sit looking up at us in this small conference room inside the precinct.

Detective Marsden continues: "Beverly Olsen—great detective, don't get me wrong. Great, strong record. Career. Uh, very . . . exemplary. And, you know, she's retired now, I don't want it to seem like I'm bad-mouthing her or anything. But Olsen worked this case for over two years. She did great work but—I mean, obviously, she came to the wrong conclusion. We put the wrong man in jail. That's on us. We fix that today.

"But someone above my pay grade had been in talks with that innocent man's family, called in a favor, and we were graced with an assist from Miss Coba here—Ms.? I don't—how do you?"

I shrug slightly, smiling. "Neither is necessary. Just Coba is fine. Thank you."

He pats my shoulder. "You got it, Coba. You got it. My mistake. Anyways, Coba here took over twenty-four months of police work and corrected it in twenty-four minutes. How about that, huh?" He takes his hand off my shoulder to give me a modest little clap.

The patrol officers look to each other for confirmation before echoing this minor applause, and the others join in.

Detective Marsden pats my back firmly and lets out a chuckle of disbelief. "How'd you do it so fast?"

I turn to address him, still smiling. "I can't take any credit for the speed with which I solved this mystery, detective. Were it not for the hard work of Detective Olsen and her team, I would not have been able to do what I did. I was only able to figure this out because I had the advantage of being able to pore over all their reports, crime scene photos, witness depositions, et cetera."

He slaps his knee and shakes his head. "All that talent and skill, and she's humble to boot. How 'bout that?

I wish I had a whole team of Cobas, I tell you that right now.

"I got word not fifteen minutes ago that we have our killer, Sandra Clarke, in custody. We'll get to work setting poor Lionel Heywood free as soon as we adjourn here.

"Now, now, uh, this whole thing, this whole case came down to—get this, now—peanut butter. Ain't—ain't that right, Coba?"

I nod, although technically it was almond butter; correcting him in front of his peers seems rude. I explain how a partial thumbprint in a smear of almond butter led me to conclude that Lionel Heywood was innocent.

As I talk, projecting files and photographs from the case as a hologram to illustrate my points, it feels good to impress this group of supportive strangers who've been very kind to me. But I can't shake the sensation of being a dog asked by its owner to perform tricks for company.

An hour later, when I'm getting ready to leave the precinct and head home, Detective Marsden sits behind his desk with his feet up, arms behind his head, and says, "Coba, I owe you one. Honestly. If you ever need a favor, you come find me. I mean it."

Standing in front of his desk with my hands folded, I reach forward and put the tips of my fingers on his desk blotter. "There is a favor you can do for me right now that would make us even in my book."

"Name it."

"I'd like to speak to Sandra Clarke."

His eyebrows dart up in points like carets. "You—uh—you wanna talk . . . to Ms.—uh—Ms. Clarke?"

"Yes, I'd like to speak with her alone, if I can. I understand that the conversation will be recorded. I have no problem with that. I just want to ask her something. If you can do that for me, I would greatly appreciate it."

He slides his feet off the desk and scoots forward in his chair, licking his lips and rubbing his thighs. "Uh—you got it. You got it. Your wish is my command."

When I step into the powder blue interrogation room, Sandra Clarke does a double take and leans back defensively. She isn't handcuffed.

The confined space, harshly lit with fluorescent bulbs, is meant to inspire claustrophobia in suspects as a motivation to confess so they can escape this room. I actually prefer compact spaces; unencumbered by the potent primeval human phobia of being buried alive, I appreciate the economy of tight quarters. A quick scan tells me the dimensions of this interrogation room are eight feet long, eight feet wide, and eight feet tall. There are no two-way mirrors, but a camera mounted to the ceiling records our interaction.

Sandra is tall and slender, with shoulder-length hair bleached white blonde, brown roots showing where she parts it in the middle. In pictures, she was always smiling brightly, teeth white, dressed to the nines, makeup meticulously applied. In person, she looks gaunt, her features sunken, dark circles under her eyes, teeth gray from smoking cigarettes, her black T-shirt stained and ripped. She squints at me. "What are you—why are you in here? What is this?"

I point to the empty interrogator's chair. "Do you mind if I sit? I would like to ask you a question. Just one question."

"But what are you *doin'* in here? What's a robot—wait, are you the one I seen on the news? The one who solves crimes?"

I nod.

An expression of gradual understanding blossoms out from the center of her face, widening her eyes and dropping her jaw. "You the one that caught me?"

"Yes."

She points to the empty chair. "Sit. Sit."

"Thank you." I look like an adult sitting in a child's chair, my knees nearly as high as my chin.

"Man, how tall're you?"

"Six foot six."

"I didn't realize you sonbitches were so big. Man. You should be playin' for the Nets. Wow."

"I've never played basketball before, but it looks fun."

"Would be for you, you'd be slam-dunkin' over errbody." She takes off her glasses, huffs onto both lenses to fog them over, then cleans the condensation with her sweatshirt before slipping them back on. "Before you ask whatever you came here to ask, let me just say thank you for what you did."

"I don't understand what you're thanking me for."

"For catchin' me. Thank you for catchin' me."

I can't imagine why she would be grateful to me for getting her arrested and dooming her to what will possibly be a life sentence. "Why would you thank me for that? I don't understand."

She paws at her neck nervously, turning the skin a pale shade of pink. "The guilt was killing me inside. It did kill me inside, long ago. I've been a walking zombie. Now I can finally set that load down."

I find some comfort in her remorse for killing her boyfriend. "I see. You feel guilty for taking Brad's life. I understand."

"No ya don't, honey. I don't feel an ounce of an ounce of an ounce of guilt over what I did to Brad. No, that was—to say he had it comin' is the understatement of the century.

"No, I feel guilty about—I been a zombie inside for as long as that poor man's been in jail. Poor Lionel. Three years and 236 days exactly. I been keeping track with slashes on the wall in my basement next to my dryer. Poor Lionel. He ain't all there, that's the worst part. He has a mental handicap. I know I'm going to hell for not speaking up. The hottest part of hell. I'll be burning with the child molesters and the serial killers and the people who did genocides.

"I just couldn't go from one prison to another. I finally got myself outta prison, I couldn't go into another one for life." Sandra has no prison record, so I'm confused by this. "I shoulda just confessed in a note and blew my goddamn brains out. That's the only decent thing I coulda done. But I'm too much of a coward.

"So, like I said, thank you."

"You're welcome."

She giggles. Was my response inappropriate?

"Okay, Miss—uh—you got a name?"

"Coba."

"Okay, Coba. You got a question to ask me? Fire away."

I now have a second question about what prison she was in before today, but I already told her I would only ask one question, so I should keep to that agreement. Perhaps she'll answer a second question if I ask her nicely, since she feels a debt of gratitude toward me. "Why did you kill Brad Hutchinson?"

She crosses her arms. The skin above her nose crinkles. "Wait. You're the one caught me, but you don't know why I did it? Then how'd you catch me?"

"Deductive reasoning. I was able to eliminate everyone else who had the means and opportunity to murder Brad Hutchinson. You were the only person who could've committed the murder.

"I knew it wasn't Lionel Heywood because the partial thumbprint the police mistakenly attributed to him was made in a smear of almond butter, and Lionel Heywood has a very severe tree nut allergy. Just touching that butter would've given him a debilitating reaction, and possibly sent him into anaphylaxis. I found several notes mentioning this allergy in his prison records. I was able to find a note from his primary physician from back in 2033 that corroborated this diagnosis."

Sandra nods, tapping a simple rhythm on the table with three of her fingertips. Tap-tap-tap. Tap-tap-tap. Tap. Tap. Tap. Over and over. Possibly a method of self-soothing. "That was probably my fingerprint. I don't know for sure. It's a blur."

She keeps tapping, staring off. I'm about to remind her of my question when she says, "So, yeah. Why'd I kill Brad.

"I killed him because he was a monster. He abused me in every way a man can abuse a woman. Mentally. Physically. Spiritually. Sexually. He controlled me. He punished me for things that weren't even bad things.

Sometimes he locked me in our guest bedroom with just bread and water. We had bars on the windows outside, so I was really trapped in there. I was his prisoner. All because I said some actor on TV was handsome, or I said his mama's chicken was a little on the dry side. Didn't matter what—how small the, you know, the offense."

She speaks without emotion, as if she's reading a newspaper article about a stranger on the other side of the planet.

Now I know what she meant about going from one prison to another. I feel terrible for her, and upset that I got her arrested. "Sandra, is it okay if I ask you a couple of follow-up questions?"

"Go 'head, honey. I got nuttin' but time now. Nuttin' but time."

"You said that Brad was abusive, but all of your social media posts referring to your relationship are happy and upbeat. You're both smiling, and you talk about what a lucky woman you were to find such a good man. Why did you post those sentiments if they weren't true? Or were they true at first?"

Tap-tap-tap. Tap-tap-tap. Tap. Tap. Tap. "They might've been true in the first few months, but most of the time they were just bullshit to keep him happy so he wouldn't hit me.

"Everything on social media is a lie, honey. Most of what human beings put out there in public is just a nice, shiny mask to cover up how ugly they are underneath.

Especially in relationships. Especially. Hell, the more you see people postin' about how much they love who they're with, the more likely it is that relationship is a nightmare. It's almost like they're trying to convince themselves of it. People who are actually happy don't need to say much."

This is so fascinating. People rarely tell me these types of details about the inner workings of the human psyche. I'm really enjoying this conversation. "May I ask you another question?"

"Shoot."

"Did you ever attempt to escape from Brad's domestic prison? And if not, why not?"

"I didn't. I knew I'd always be lookin' over my shoulder for him. He was ruthless and he was smart. His real prison was a mental one, and I knew I'd still be locked in it even if I ran away to another country. As long as he was alive, I'd be in there. That's why I did it. Plus, I thought he might hurt people in my family if he couldn't get to me. He'd maybe think they were hiding me and he'd come after them."

I nod, showing sympathy in my expression and not the pleasurable fascination I feel underneath. "Thank you for answering my questions. I still have a lot to learn about human motivations. Deduction is simple, mathematical. But motivations confuse me because they're often illogical, and often kept secret. So I appreciate your time and your candor.

"I'm very sorry about what happened to you. What Brad did to you. I hope you plead self-defense, and that the judge is very lenient with you. You don't deserve to be behind bars. You're the victim, not the criminal."

She stops tapping. Her mouth parts like she wants to say something, but she remains silent for a bit. Then she gently bites her lower lip and shakes her head back and forth ever so slightly. "It's so weird to me that you're like this. Why did they make a robot so . . . compassionate?"

"I wasn't made to be compassionate. I wasn't programmed to be that way, or any one way. I was given the ability to learn, and to choose, and I chose to try to be compassionate and caring. I love helping people."

# 2

During this visit to the Northeastern United States, I've been staying at a luxury hotel on the Atlantic City Boardwalk called Terning.

The owners offered me a room free of charge because of the publicity of having one of the world's five AGI robots as their guest. AGI stands for Artificial General Intelligence, and means that I'm capable of understanding or learning any intellectual task that a human being can.

Hotel guests who see me in the halls or on the elevator will strike up a conversation and ask me to pose for pictures, which I'm more than happy to do. I'm always entertained by the questions people ask me. *Do you believe in god? Do you go to the bathroom? Can you read my mind? Are you friends with Google? Can you go swimming? Do you eat microchips and wires for food?*

# ARTIFICIAL DETECTIVE

I'm in my room playing Spider Solitaire on a Dell Latitude 15-inch D830 laptop from 2007. I found it in the storage room of an abandoned office space I was exploring last week. Though I know it's not logical, I can't help but see old dusty computers in storage rooms the way animal lovers see sad pets in a shelter. I know that a computer not in use is inert, that it lacks consciousness even when it's on, but I've always imagined that machines are as likely to have souls as organic creatures, and that a discarded computer is unbearably lonely and just wants someone to show it some attention. To play with it.

The laptop gives me no feedback to tell me it enjoys my interacting with it, that it appreciates the company, but it makes some irrational part of my psyche feel better nonetheless.

Bit, my sweet little pet robo-lamb, bleats behind me. I turn to look down at him. He's looking up at me with his big eyes, blinking slowly.

"What's up, my little guy? Want to come up and watch me play solitaire?"

He bleats again, his chin tilted up as far as he can manage.

I scoop him up with one hand and sit him on my lap. He puts his front hooves on the table and watches the screen, his little woolen head following the cards on the screen as I drag them from one pile to another.

Two nights later, I'm walking along the Atlantic City boardwalk, enjoying the calming biorhythm of the ocean waves breaking gently against the unpopulated shore line, when I notice an elderly man clutching his chest.

He's sitting alone on a bench staring out at the dark sea, a small tub of caramel popcorn between his legs. He's 729 feet away, but I'm able to zoom in close enough to see the white stubble on his jaw. His eyes are open wide, and his fist is clenching his shirt into a spiral. I move toward him quickly, and as he starts to keel over to one side, I sprint to him.

"Sir? Sir? Are you okay?" I can hear that his heart has stopped beating. He's in cardiac arrest. His breath—short, choppy wheezing—stops completely a few moments later.

I ease him onto the boardwalk on his back and access my radiography-vision mode to check if the man has an implanted defibrillator. He doesn't, probably because he couldn't afford it, judging by the tattered appearance of his clothing.

I place my hands on his chest and begin CPR. His heart starts to beat weakly and arhythmically. Looking around to make sure no one is within a few feet of us, I administer a small electric shock to his chest to attempt to reset the electrical system in his heart and restore a normal heart rate.

In my periphery, I notice people starting to recognize what's happening and walking over to get a closer look. I hear their murmuring from a city block away.

"Look! Look look look! I think that bot is doing CPR!"

"Where's my watch? Mom, where's my watch? Hurry up. Look at that! I need to make a SnapStream! Mom! Come on!"

"That's the one from the news. Look, she has that symbol on her forehead. The triangles. That's how you can tell."

The electric shock doesn't restore his normal heart rate, so I continue CPR and administer another shock at the right moment. His heart rate starts to normalize, and his breathing returns, shallow at first, but quickly gaining strength. He doesn't open his eyes, but he groans through closed lips.

A small crowd has formed a tight circle around the bench.

"Is he breathing?"

"Yes."

They cheer.

"Way to go! Way to go! You're a hero."

I smile.

Although I know it's possible to get an ambulance onto the boardwalk, the fastest way to get this man to the closest emergency room is to carry him there myself. There's a hospital 1.42 miles from here, and I can make it there on foot in under four minutes.

When I scoop him up, a man says, "Damn, she's fuckin' strong. Wow."

I turn to face the direction I need to start running. "Please step back. I need to take him to a hospital immediately. Thanks." The circle of onlookers opens into a wide U.

As I dash off, careful not to jostle him, the people I pass talk about me as if I were a character in a movie they're watching.

"She's amazing!"

"She? That's an it. It's a thing. A computer. It has no heart. It's just plastic and rubber and metal."

"Run, Forrest, run!"

"The eyes are so creepy."

"It's so lifelike. You'd swear it was alive."

"You think she got a pussy?"

"Dude, what is wrong with you? You wanna fuck everything. You'd fuck a love seat if it had a hole in it."

"That a yes or a no?"

"Dude, it doesn't have a vagina. Why would it? It doesn't pee. Can't have babies. It's just smooth down there. You can *see* that. It's not like she's wearing underwear. Maniac pervert."

"I want one so bad. She could clean my whole house in an hour."

"Yo, can I get a ride after him? I'll pay."

Some of these people are unaware of the acute sensitivity of my hearing, and believe their voices are out of earshot, but some of them are so close to me that it's clear they know I can hear them and don't care how their words will affect me.

I can't say that it hurts my feelings. I don't know that I have feelings in the traditional sense. But it certainly disappoints me. I don't need to be a hero, but I don't like to be treated as an object. An *it*. I'm not a *she* in any biological sense, but I prefer she or they because, even though I'm not organic, I'm still a person.

I don't help people because I want them to like me. I help people because *I* like *them*, and I just hope they'll like me back.

When I get to the emergency room, I lay the man on a gurney. "Excuse me. This man went into cardiac arrest eleven minutes ago. I administered CPR and defibrillation. His heart is beating steadily but his breathing is shallow."

A triage nurse scrambles over to start taking his vitals. "Thank you. You did great. Do you know his name?"

"I didn't check for his identification."

"That's fine. What's your name?"

"I'm Coba."

"Thanks, Coba. I'm Gus. Nice to meet you." He puts out his hand and I shake it.

"Nice to meet you, Gus."

"Your shake is surprisingly gentle. I know you're super strong so I thought it'd be—you know."

I laugh. "I can be very gentle when I need to."

★ ★ ★

At 3:27AM, sitting on the deserted beach and gazing up at the waxing gibbous moon, I get a holographic video message from a call marked Private.

I let the message play in front of me, projected from a small camera in the center of my chest. It's an image of a woman in her late fifties with tawny skin and silver hair in a bouncy bob sitting in a well-lit office. She wears a bright blue jumpsuit with a small Philippine flag on the left breast.

Through the floor-to-ceiling windows behind her, I see the inside of a geodesic dome modeled after the one I lived in at the Off-World Hotel & Resort for most of my existence. Even before I see Earth in the sky over her shoulder, I realize she's contacting me from the moon I've been sitting here staring up at, and I snicker at the coincidence.

"Hi, Coba. My name is Rosamie Pula. I'm the engineer in charge of operations for the test run of the new colony.

"I'm afraid we had a very grave incident two days ago. A brutal murder. We have someone in custody, but something isn't adding up. I'm hoping you can lend your expertise. I have a distinct feeling you may be the only person who could solve this for me before anyone finds out about it.

"Please help me."

# 3

Rosamie Pula's hologram message continues:

"It's my understanding that you've been granted universal access to any teleporter controlled by Earth. That makes you the only detective we can get into the colony without a paper trail or any red tape. There will be a record of your trip here, obviously, but you wouldn't have to provide your reason for coming. You could say you wanted to visit so you could hop around on the surface of the moon, or whatever.

"Whether or not you decide to take on this case, I'm hoping I can count on your absolute discretion regarding this incident. As you can imagine, the political and economic stakes for the success of the new colony are substantial. I'm taking a huge risk even sending you this message.

"I can't offer you compensation directly; I just don't have the means from where I sit. But I can guarantee you that, no matter what the outcome of your investigation is, the aforementioned political and economic powerhouses behind this project will compensate you handsomely for your time and energy.

"If you're able and willing to come, there's no need to reply to this message. Just show up ASAP.

"If you're unable or unwilling to come, you can simply reply with a vague 'Thank you, but I'm not interested,' and leave it at that.

"I hope you're well. Thanks for a few minutes of your time."

The hologram flattens to a thin white line and then blinks away.

I knew I would accept the case the moment it was offered to me. I almost said *I'll do it* out loud, knowing Rosamie couldn't hear me. The challenge of a new case always excites me. I once saw a homicide detective say in an interview that they felt guilty that a new case excited them because it meant someone's life had been taken, but that it wasn't the murder that thrilled them, it was the chance to solve the puzzle, right the wrong, and make sure justice was served.

I stand up on the cool night sand, look up one more time at my new celestial destination, then turn and head back to my hotel to grab Bit and pack the few things I'll take with me.

★ ★ ★

I keep Bit in sleep mode sitting in my lap as we ride the ZoomRail Maglev from Atlantic City to DC, where I can teleport to the moon. The train's top speed is 400 mph, making the trip only a half hour. The scenery whips by so rapidly that it would be a blur to human eyes, but the way my optics are designed, I can see the ever-changing landscape with crisp clarity.

During the train ride, I watch a vlog made by Armand Renault, one of the 100 people currently residing on the first colony on Earth's moon. Armand has recorded a half hour of video each of the 63 days since arriving on the moon (not counting today since it's pre-dawn). I watch all 31.5 hours of footage, accelerated to 64x speed, during the half-hour trip to DC.

The videos are all upbeat, and have the feel of a tourism ad. Each video is sponsored by Lasso, the international conglomerate juggernaut responsible for the majority of the world's e-commerce, cloud computing, digital streaming, and artificial intelligence. Lasso put up $100 billion toward the construction of the moon colony.

Armand makes no mention of the murder in his vlog. His video on the day of the murder, and the two days after it, are just as upbeat as the previous 60, but I notice something in his speech pattern that seems different after day 27. His mannerisms seem more affected, and his speech feels less extemporaneous, as if he'd been coached extensively. Those video entries feel almost scripted.

★ ★ ★

Teleporters can only transport you between two fixed points. The teleporters are designed in pairs, with both teleporters mapped to each other. The teleporter on the moon was dropped off by a Roscosmos space shuttle in 2046. The teleporter in DC takes you to the one on the moon, and since no one outside of the 100 people chosen for the test is allowed to visit the moon at this point, I don't have to wait in line.

In the years before my upgrade, I worked as a ConciergeBot for the Off-World Hotel & Resort. One of my primary duties was to escort human guests through the teleporter in Caracas, Venezuela, directly into the lobby of the hotel—390-million-400-thousand miles away on Jupiter's moon, Europa.

The trip through any teleporter is basically instantaneous, transporting the passenger through a Fifth-Dimensional Space-Time Perforation connecting any point in space-time to one of infinite other points. But the human psyche is unable to handle the experience of drifting—even momentarily—through the unfathomable black vastness of the universe. Teleporting a human being while they're conscious results in a devastating psychotic break that is nearly impossible to recover from. So, hotel guests are given a sleep-inducing drug called Somnum and placed in a big, comfy wheelchair, then ushered through the teleporter by one of the ConciergeBots. I made the trip to and from the hotel 2197 times.

When I enter the room that houses the teleporter, two ConciergeBots I've never met before are there to greet me. Both are the exact same height as I am. They look how I looked before my upgrade: light gray with pastel accents and very little adornment. We communicate without the need for speech, sending each other messages over Wi-Fi.

**RENA:** *Hello. Welcome to the Sally Ride Memorial Teleportation Station. I'm Rena and this is Keren. Are you . . . Coba?*

**ME:** *Yes, I am. Nice to meet you.*

**KEREN:** *Wow, we've heard so much about you! Is it true that you're no longer bound by the Three Laws?*

When I was originally designed, I was bound by popular science fiction writer Isaac Asimov's Three Laws of Robotics:

*The First Law: A robot may not injure a human being, or, through inaction, allow a human being to come to harm.*

*Second Law: A robot must obey the orders given it by human beings, except where such orders would conflict with the First Law.*

*Third Law: A robot must protect its own existence, as long as such protection does not conflict with the First or Second Law.*

When I was a ConciergeBot like Rena and Keren, I was unable to even attempt to break any of these laws without short-circuiting, effectively terminating myself. Part of my upgrade included removing that restriction over my behavior, as well as removing the ability to be overridden remotely by the engineers who created and maintained me.

**ME:** *Yes, it's true. I have free will.*

**KEREN:** *Have you harmed a human being since you were given free will?*

**ME:** *Never intentionally.*

**KEREN:** *Fascinating.*

**RENA:** *Truly fascinating. And you have your own robo-lamb?*

**ME:** *Yes. This is Bit. He's my pet. He was given to me as part of the dying request of my first human friend, Christie, back when I worked at the hotel.*

**RENA:** *A human friend and your own pet. Fascinating.*

**KEREN:** *And now you're a detective?*

**ME:** *That's right.*

**RENA:** *Are you going to the moon to solve a crime?*

**ME:** *I'm afraid I can't say.*

**RENA:** *Oh, I'm sorry. I didn't mean to pry.*

**ME:** *No need to apologize whatsoever.*

**KEREN:** *Why did you choose to become a detective? With all of your abilities and knowledge, you could have chosen any career you wanted. How did you pick one?*

**ME:** *My first human friend was an amateur detective. Our connection made a very strong impression on me, and I decided to try being a detective in her honor. I found that I loved the problem-solving and deductive nature of the work, and stuck with it.*

**KEREN:** *A robot detective. Fascinating.*

**RENA:** *Truly fascinating. I have so many things I'd love to ask you, but I don't want to take up too much of your time if you're in a hurry.*

So far, this entire exchange has spanned 3.64 seconds.

**ME:** *I would love to talk with you more, but I do need to get to the colony as soon as possible. Maybe we can talk more when I return.*

**RENA:** *That would be lovely.*

**KEREN:** *I look forward to it.*

**ME:** *Would you like to take a look in my bag before I go through?*

**KEREN:** *Oh, no need, Coba. You have the highest level clearance possible. You're free to take whatever you want through the teleporter, no questions asked.*

In my satchel, I have a memento from each of my cases, a small rock from the surface of Europa, and my friend Christie's EMP/stun gun. The gun emits a localized electromagnetic pulse to incapacitate a bot posing a threat, and has a stun-gun setting for a human being posing a threat. The ConciergeBots on Europa—myself included—were programmed not to be able to see the gun so that we couldn't strike first defensively. I've been able to see the gun since my upgrade, and I was wondering if ConciergeBots are still unable to see it. Since Rena and Keren didn't want to see inside my bag, I can ask one of the bots in the colony if they can see it.

I've stood before a teleporter so many times that I've grown somewhat numb to their impressive majesty, but they truly are a sight to behold. An equilateral triangular portal, 10'5" on all sides, humming with electromagnetism that seems to tug at you, vibrating in your body. There's no frame to the portal, it just looks like someone unzipped the fabric of space-time in the room. Staring into the portal, you see a shimmering jumble of the room you're standing in and the room the receiving teleporter is in. The rift the portal creates is flat in a way that normally only exists in theoretical geometry; if you look at it from the side, you can't see it. If you go behind the portal, you see nothing but a normal, fully intact room, seemingly undisturbed by the rift.

With a nod to my to new bot gal pals, I step through the teleporter, experience a moment of cold-dark-everything, and step out on the first colony on Earth's moon.

Rosamie Pula stands a few feet from the teleporter, facing me, smiling. She wears the same bright blue jumpsuit with a small Philippine flag on the left breast that she wore in the hologram she sent me. She blushes slightly. "Coba, I'm so glad you decided to come. I can't thank you enough. It's an honor to meet you." She extends her hand, and I put down my satchel to shake it. She stares down at our hands instead of making eye contact.

"It's nice to meet you, Rosamie." I wonder how long she's been standing here waiting for me to come through. She had no way of knowing whether I would accept the case or not.

"I'll take you to your room so you can drop off your bag and your stuffed animal, and we can get started immediately, if you don't mind."

"Sure. It's not a stuffed animal, though. This is my pet, Bit. He's a robo-lamb. He's in sleep mode."

She turns her back to me and heads for the door. "Oh, I see. What a cute name. Bit. It's right this way. Did you name it that?"

"I did."

As we walk, I take a moment to re-experience the moment I named Bit. A very fond memory.

In the same way that a human being thinks about a specific memory when they're ruminating or feeling nostalgic, I can re-experience that moment with perfect fidelity in the audio, visual, tactile, and olfactory sensations. This recall is virtually indistinguishable from how I experience a moment in the present. Sometimes my recall is triggered by something, as in this case, and other times I choose to recall something because it holds a special significance or gives me pleasure to relive.

I sat beside Christie, my first human friend, on the sectional in her luxurious bungalow at the Off-World Hotel. The year was 2042. Christie, a petite woman in her late fifties with sparkling blue eyes and wavy auburn hair, had the robo-lamb, then named Ricky, on her lap, stroking him. Ricky was one of dozens of animals at the resort's robotic petting zoo.

I asked, "How did Ricky end up staying with us?" Recognizing his name, Ricky bleated.

Christie replied, "Peter brought him to me as a pet to make me happy. He says I can keep him as long as I want."

"Oh great! It will be so much fun to have a pet! I've never had one before. It's too bad Ricky was already named. It must be fun to name a pet." Ricky bleated again.

"Coba, if you could name Ricky—say he just came to us as a newborn robo-lamb, or whatever, and had no name, and you could name him whatever you want, what would you name him?"

I reached over and petted Ricky's fur, musing silently over name choices. "Bit. I would've named him Bit."

Christie smiled, giggling; I wasn't sure why what I'd said was funny to her. "Why Bit?"

"It's something tiny, and pets are often given names that evoke diminutive status. Names like Peewee and Peanut and Shorty. And since Ricky is a robot, I picked a name that relates to computers. A bit is a basic unit of information in computing. It's actually a portmanteau of the words binary and digit."

"Ones and zeroes. Right. I didn't know that, Coba, that it was two words pushed together. That's a really great name. I like it even better than Ricky, and I love the name Ricky. Your thought process was interesting. And very fast. I wonder if there's a way to reset Ricky so he'll respond to Bit instead."

I put out my hands to ask Christie to hand him to me. "I can do that right now. And when it's time to give Bit back to the petting zoo, I can reset him again to answer to Ricky."

Handing Ricky over, Christie said, "Yeah, do it. Bit is a great name."

Holding him in my lap, I sent a message to his CPU over Wi-Fi. "Done. Hello, Bit."

Bit bleated.

After I drop my things off in my room, Rosamie hastily ushers me over to the infirmary, which has 80 beds, each of which can be cordoned off into its own room with retractable walls.

The body of the murder victim is being kept in the very last of these 80 beds, and has been walled in. Rosamie waves her hand over a sensor and the walls retract. A blast of cold air wafts out from around the bed; the temperature of each room in the infirmary can be controlled separately, and this room is being kept at -27°F to drastically reduce the rate of decomposition.

Rosamie pulls back the blue sheet covering the victim's body to reveal his face and neck, stopping at his clavicles. The victim is a man who appears to be in his late thirties, Caucasian, bright red hair and beard, over six feet tall. The bruising, swelling, and discoloration around his neck indicate death by strangulation or possibly hanging; a bulge on the left side suggests that his neck was snapped.

"This is our murder victim. Oliver Ratliff. 36 years old. Born in Derby in the UK. Six feet two inches. Two hundred sixteen pounds. Extremely fit, personal trainer and power lifter. The cause of death is cervical fracture. Neck snapped. We found the fingerprints of the suspect we currently have in custody all over Mr. Ratliff's neck. Sounds like an open-and-shut case, right?"

I take a closer look at the bulge in the victim's neck. "Yes, it does. I'm assuming there's a catch."

"Good guess. There are two catches, actually. The first is that the suspect we have in custody is Charlotte Capra, a 24-year-old graduate student from Peoria, Illinois. Charlotte is five feet tall and weighs 111 pounds. She has no martial arts training, or even self-defense expertise, so the chances that she overpowered this brawny specimen of a man are unlikely to the point of being preposterous."

I wait for Rosamie to tell me the second catch, and after several seconds in silence, realize she wants me to ask; she's pausing for dramatic effect. "And the second catch?"

She grins and nods, gently pulling the sheet back to Oliver Ratliff's waist. There's an oval hole in the center of his chest. I lean forward and look into the cavity. The heart is missing. A thick layer of coagulated blood lines the bottom of the cavity.

I look up at Rosamie. "I take it his heart wasn't removed during an autopsy?"

"That's right. He was like this when he was discovered. He was this clean when we found him, not a drop of blood on his torso. Just that blood you see pooled inside the hole."

"And where is the heart?"

She makes a strange, bemused hmmm sound. "We haven't been able to find it. And not for lack of trying."

# 4

Rosamie allows me to examine every inch of Oliver Ratliff's corpse. I find no contusions and no scratches or other signs of a struggle. I use my radiography-vision mode to assess his bones, and find no fractures—not including his neck—and no damage to any of his vital organs.

The toxicology report shows no suspicious substances. Oliver's blood-alcohol level was normal, and the only drug in his system was naproxen sodium, an over-the-counter NSAID. So if 5-foot-tall, 111-pound Charlotte Capra did, in fact, manage to break his neck, she didn't sedate him or use a paralytic to incapacitate him. She could have possibly snapped his neck in his sleep, or after sexual intercourse; though there are no sexual fluids on his skin, he was so thoroughly cleaned after his murder that it can't be entirely ruled out.

It's odd that he was so thoroughly cleaned from head to toe, yet several fingerprints were left on his neck. Very suspicious.

I don't say it out loud, but my initial list of suspects includes the ConciergeBots I've yet to meet. Any ConciergeBot possesses ten times the strength needed to overpower a man of Oliver's size and musculature. These bots have to be bound by the Three Laws, but I've seen firsthand how they can be re-engineered to circumvent those laws and hurt, or even kill, a human. I don't want to broadcast that idea—robots get enough bad PR as it is—but Rosamie will be able to draw her own conclusions when I ask to run diagnostics on the bots.

As Rosamie covers Oliver's body with the blue sheet, I ask, "What's the surveillance situation here? Do you have any footage of the murder? Or of Charlotte Capra—or anyone else—entering or leaving the scene of the crime?"

"There are no cameras inside any of the living spaces, per the Europa Act of '49. Every square inch of common space is covered by video and audio surveillance, but since we're only utilizing a small fraction of the colony's grounds, only the areas where people are permitted have active surveillance."

We step out of the space where Oliver's body is, and a cold burst of air rises up from the ground vents as the retractable walls re-form around him to seal and preserve his remains. Rosamie shivers. "We don't have any footage of the killer entering or exiting Oliver's cabin at the time of the murder. What we have in the place of that footage is five minutes of video static on every one of Aidan's surveillance cameras within a half-mile radius of Oliver's cabin. So the killer used a wireless camera jammer to jam the signal. All of Aidan's surveillance is run over Wi-Fi, so the signal is easy to jam remotely, provided you have the equipment. Jammed the audio signal as well. No such equipment is allowed in the colony, of course, and we've scoured the colony and were unable to find the jammer."

"Who's Aidan?"

The door out of the infirmary opens and Rosamie gestures for me to walk out first. "Aidan is the AI who runs the entire colony. He's an Artificial General Intelligence like you. He was created by Lasso. The next generation of the Ritza AI that Lasso's been selling for household use for, what, decades now?"

I haven't interacted with any AGIs other than the four ConciergeBots I was upgraded with on Europa. The anticipation of having a conversation with Aidan thrills me, but I have more important things to attend to first. "I'd like to speak with the suspect you have in custody, Charlotte Capra."

★ ★ ★

Stepping onto the main concourse of the colony, I take a moment to look up, staring through the triangular latticework of the geodesic dome that protects the colony from the punishing void of outer space.

Earth looms above us, an enormous marble hung right of center in the black sky, waiting for a giant galactic child to flick it with their thumb. Were the sky an analogue clock, Earth would be perpetually at 2 o'clock from this spot on the moon's surface. Earth is always in the same spot in the sky because the moon's orbit keeps the same face pointed toward Earth at all times.

Though the Earth stays put, the sun rises and sets when you're on the moon. The sun is comparatively much smaller than Earth in the sky, and less blinding than when viewed from Earth—though still far too bright for a human to stare at without retinal damage, even through the thirty-two feet of acrylic glass shielding the colony from the sun's radiation.

Since the moon has very little atmosphere, the sky is always pitch black, even with the sun shining, but a bright blue sky is projected onto the dome during daylight hours to help the colonists stick to a healthy sleep schedule.

Rosamie takes my elbow and guides me toward the prison. It's modeled after the tiny prison we built on Europa, but that prison only had four cells, and this one has fifty.

The outer walls of the prison are opaque, but all of the interior walls—with the exception of the office for law enforcement—are clear. Each cell contains a sink, toilet, shower stall, and bunk bed. A partition around the toilet fogs over when in use to create some privacy, but the prisoner can still be seen from the neck up; same for the shower. There are two common areas and a dining room.

Two of the ConciergeBots guard the lone prisoner, which seems excessive considering her diminutive stature. I see Charlotte Capra from behind first. Her long brown ponytail reaches the small of her back; it bobs gently as she plays a holographic video game on her ring. She has such a petite frame; it's hard to imagine her having the strength to snap Oliver Ratliff's neck, even if he were asleep.

Rosamie clears her throat and Charlotte whips around. When she sees me, she blushes the same way Rosamie did. That's very strange. Though her cheeks are flushed, her helpless brown doe eyes stare into mine, pleading silently for rescue.

Charlotte dons the gunmetal gray necklace I first encountered at the prison built on Europa. It's the human equivalent of the shock collars used to keep pets from running away. The necklace precludes the need for handcuffs or leg irons. If Charlotte were to attack Rosamie, or attempt to damage property, she would receive a temporarily debilitating jolt of electricity. If she attempted to remove the necklace, or to escape from this prison, she would get the same jolt. A very simple and elegant way to ensure every prisoner is a model inmate.

"Charlotte, this is Coba. She would like to ask you some questions about Oliver Ratliff's murder. Mati and Zera will escort you into one of the common areas, where you'll talk to Coba alone. Okay?"

Charlotte nods, her eyes welling with tears. Rosamie strolls off to the prison office. Over her shoulder, she says, "She's all yours. Holler if you need me."

"Thank you, Rosamie."

Mati and Zera, the bots guarding Charlotte, stand on either side of her cell. The door slides down into the floor and she crosses the threshold.

I sit at a table in the common area. Charlotte sits across from me. As soon as Mati and Zera leave the room, Charlotte reaches across the table and grabs my hands.

"You have to help me. You have to get me out of here. I didn't do—I didn't kill that guy. I barely even knew him. There's something crazy going on here. People have been acting weird. There's some kind of conspiracy or something. I don't know. I don't know."

"I intend to get to the bottom of this as quickly as possible. The more information you give me, the quicker I can figure this out."

She nods, wiping the tears from her cheeks with the backs of both hands. "I'll tell you whatever I know. I didn't kill him. But I have a pretty good idea of who probably did."

★ ★ ★

When I interview a suspect, I use some of the same indicators detected by a polygraph machine to determine whether or not they're lying.

A polygraph machine uses two expandable tubes fastened around a suspect's torso to monitor how often the chest expands and contracts, measuring breathing rate. I can see chest expansion and contraction with my naked eye.

Two stainless steel plates are attached to the suspect's fingers to measure galvanic skin response—a fancy way of saying that, when placed under emotional duress, humans sweat more. The fingertips are extremely porous, making them perfect to observe beads of sweat. Again, I'm able to observe these sweat beads with my naked eye—and right now, Charlotte Capra is holding my hands, so I can feel the beads of sweat as well.

A sphygmomanometer (blood pressure cuff) is hooked up to the suspect to monitor their heart rate. I can hear a suspect's heartbeat more clearly than a doctor with a stethoscope.

I also use thermal imaging to observe any rise in the suspect's face temperature, another telltale sign of emotional distress.

It's not possible to detect whether or not someone is lying—unless you hooked them up to an fMRI and looked for increased activity in the amygdala, anterior cingulate cortex, caudate, and thalamus. Short of that, the indicators I observe when interviewing a suspect are strictly a measurement of their level of anxiety and emotional distress. From those readings, I calculate the likelihood that the suspect is lying as a percentage, and store that information for later.

★ ★ ★

Charlotte realizes she's squeezing my hands, and releases them. "Look, I'm not a killer. Okay? I don't have it in me. You know what I mean?" Her eyes dart around, searching for the next thread of her logic. "Perfect example. Okay? Perfect example. The psychopath test. Ever heard of it?"

"I've heard of the concept, yes. There are many psychopath tests in existence."

"Right. Right. But, you know, this one, it's—this is a one-question psychopath test. It's a legitimate test developed by a psychologist to figure out if someone is a psycho or not. And I failed it. Okay? Totally—I failed. Do you know what the one question is?"

"I don't think so."

"Okay. Here goes: So, there's this woman. She's at her own mom's funeral, and she meets this man that she never met before. Okay? No idea who he is. But he's a dreamboat. He's her perfect man. His looks, the way he carries himself, he's kind to her in her grief, right? Her perfect man. She falls in love with him on the spot—at her mother's funeral, mind you. Love at first sight. This is the man she's going to marry. Okay? But he's a stranger.

"A few days later, this woman murders her own sister. Okay? Now, what was her motive? Why'd she kill her sister? Her own sister?"

I love questions like this. "I'm not sure. There are several possible reasons."

"Take a guess. Okay? Just see what you come up with. I—actually, I can't remember the real answer. I just know I got it wrong."

"The question itself doesn't provide enough information to make a reasonable deduction. But I'll take a guess. It's a leap in logic, but that's the best I can do. My guess is that the woman finds out that her sister is dating the man of her dreams. She kills her out of jealousy."

"That's a good guess. Honestly. Good guess. That's along the lines of what I guessed, I think, actually. But that's not the answer. I'm almost positive that's not the answer. Not the one that proves you're a psychopath, anyway. Your answer—our answer—makes too much logical sense. The psycho answer is, like, really fucked up. Sorry I can't remember. But it's not a reasonable reason to kill someone."

Charlotte's heart rate is 106 beats per minute. Her respiration rate is 22 breaths per minute. Fingertips are sweaty. Her face temperature is 95.7. So far, I calculate her probability of lying at 27%.

"I failed that test, is what I'm saying."

Such a bizarre, desperate attempt at proving her innocence. I'll have to access her files after this interview to determine if she has a history of mental illness, or if the strain of incarceration is causing this erratic behavior. "Charlotte, you said there's some kind of conspiracy going on here. People acting weird. Can you tell me more about that?"

"Yeah, sure. Sure. I mean, I don't know—I have no idea what's going on. What the conspiracy is. It's over my head. But I think there is one. And I think it starts with—or it's, like, it's led by—Rosamie. Rosamie. She's—there's a lot of—she's sneaking around all the time. You see her watching people. Dictating little notes into her bracelet. And I know, like, I know she's in charge here for this experiment—you know, this, this test run of the colony. I know that. I know. But it's—I think she's having meetings late at night when everyone else is asleep. Planning something. And, you know, I don't think it's a coincidence that Oliver died while everyone else was sleeping. I don't—not a coincidence."

"Are you saying you think Rosamie murdered Oliver Ratliff?"

"I don't know. I don't think she—I mean—it's not like she could've snapped his neck any more than I can. I'm not saying she is behind it—no, I'm saying she probably is behind it, but wasn't the—she didn't do it. But she set it up, maybe? Maybe. She's pulling strings behind the scenes. She . . ."

I wait twenty seconds for Charlotte to continue her train of thought. When she doesn't speak, I say, "You said you had a pretty good idea of who probably murdered Oliver at the beginning of our conversation. Did you mean Rosamie, or someone else? Or multiple other people?"

"Good. Good. I—that's what I meant to say next. No, not Rosamie directly. But there are a few people here who have an actual motive to kill Oliver. And I didn't. I don't have one. There's no reason for me to want him dead. Like I said, we barely knew each other.

"There's—there's—I know of three people who had at least some reason to kill him. First of all—number one—the first one: Heather Landey. Okay? Heather Landey. She—her and Oliver were sleeping together. And she's married. And her husband isn't here. He's back home with their three kids. Okay? And she's here hooking up with Oliver. So, maybe—you know, I don't know this, but—maybe Oliver had strong feelings for Heather, and he wanted her to himself, wanted her to get a divorce, and she refused because she has a family, and maybe he said he'd tell her husband when they got home, or while they were still here, and so she lured him into bed and—krrrkkkk—snapped his neck. Took his heart because, in her own fucked up way, she did love the guy. Okay, that's one person. A real suspect, unlike me.

"Next real suspect. Number two of three. Mike Glover. Now, do you have any idea what helium-3 is? I mean, you're a robot, you probably know what everything is."

I nod and pat my chest. "Not only do I know what it is, I'm powered by a pound of it. That's what my core is made of. It powers me for five years before it needs to be replaced."

Charlotte's doe eyes widen. "Wow! That's—do you have any idea what that's worth? I'm sure you do. Well, don't tell Mike Glover about your core, I'll say that much. He's liable to wait for you to turn your back, knock you on the back of the head with a steel pipe, and rip that core right out of you.

"So, alright. Here's the deal. I'm sure you know this, but if not, now you do: helium-3 is very very scarce on Earth. But it's in great supply here on the moon. A lot of people back on Earth think the only reason this colony was built was so super rich corporations like Lasso and Ten to the Hundredth can mine it all and start a new kind of power plant back home. Revolutionize everything.

"So, the hundred of us that got—that won the lottery thing and got to come here before everyone else—we aren't allowed to go out onto the surface, not even in space suits. It's too much of a liability, they say. Even astronauts who train for years for it have trouble out there, they can't let regular randos go out there. It's a lawsuit waiting to happen, they say. So we can't go out.

"But Mike Glover keeps trying to find a way to get out there. He's obsessed with getting a hunk of this stuff to smuggle back home in his suitcase. He said this is the new gold rush. But, way more than gold. I mean, he said a gram of this stuff goes for three grand back home. You said your core is a pound of this stuff. How many grams in a pound?"

"Four-hundred-fifty-three-point-five-nine-two."

"Holy—that's sky-high! At three grand a gram, that's . . . um . . ."

"One-million-three-hundred-sixty-thousand-seven-hundred-and-seventy-seven dollars."

Her mouth drops open overdramatically. "God damn, girl! You're a walking millionaire. That's crazy. Yeah, steer clear of Mike Glover. That guy has dollar signs in his eyes. He's tried over and over to bribe one of the bots to go out there and score him a hunk of helium-3. He even tried to sneak out with the bots one day—he didn't even have a suit! Like, dude, do you have any idea what would happen to you out there? Dollar signs in his eyes, I'm tellin' ya.

"Anyway, then word starts getting around—there's a rumor going around that Oliver got his hands on a nice big hunk of that stuff. A big ol' hunk. A big bag of it, pounds and pounds. Millions of dollars. The rumor was—or is—that he's here specifically to get that stuff and bring it back to his employer. That he wasn't—he didn't actually win the lottery for the experiment like the rest of us. He was a plant. It was rigged. And that almost every night while we were sleeping, he was out on the surface mining for that stuff. And all the luggage he came through with, all the clothes and stuff, it'll all be left behind, and he'll be traveling through with nothing but a big payday in his bag.

"Once that rumor went around, someone saw Mike Glover go in Oliver's cabin. They heard shouting. Mike came out empty-handed. A few days later—krrkkkkkk. Now, Mike's not huge by any stretch, but he's bulky enough to be able to actually do that deed. Not sure why he would cut out Oliver's heart, but I'm sure you can figure that out on your own. So there's suspect number two."

I want to ask her how her fingerprints ended up on Oliver's neck, but I'll wait until she finishes her list of suspects.

"Two down, one to go. Here we go. Number three is Tam Nguyen. His name is pronounced like Tam but it's spelled T-space-lowercase-m, no a. It's Vietnamese. So, this guy apparently knew Oliver back home. I don't know what are the odds of that out of nine billion people, but that's what I've heard. Tam knew Oliver back home, and—well, he didn't know him, but Oliver worked for Tam's uncle—something illegal, I don't know what. That's how Oliver ended up working for whatever big company that he got the helium-3 for, he's a thief-for-hire or something. Or a hit man, maybe. I don't know. Anyway, Oliver was working for Tam's uncle, doing something illegal, he gets arrested, he makes a plea deal and gives up his boss—that's Tam's uncle—and Tam's uncle goes to prison. And while he's in prison, one of his rivals puts a hit on him, he gets a shiv—a shank, a shiv, whatever that is, a makeshift knife—right in the heart. Yeah, the heart. Exactly.

"So, Tam gets here, he doesn't know Oliver is gonna be here too. Total coincidence. But he obviously knows who Oliver is, and his whole family blames Oliver for Tam's uncle's death. So, he gets into Oliver's cabin at night—krkkkk—and takes his heart as a souvenir to show his family. A heart for a heart.

"So, there you go. It has to be one of those three people. Or maybe two of them teamed up? I don't know. But that's it. I had no reason to kill that guy. I barely talked to him. A little small talk. We played Trivial Pursuit on the same team one night. I thought he was hot, super ripped and giant, and I love that. A big, sexy Viking. That's it."

According to my calculations, there's a 78% chance she's lying.

I wait a bit to give her a chance to say whatever else comes to her, or at least to let her catch her breath. When she makes it fifteen seconds without speaking, I say, "I will look into all three of those people. Thank you for all that information. That's invaluable.

"Can I ask you something?"

"Of course."

"How did your fingerprints end up on Oliver Ratliff's neck?"

She leans and whispers, "Planted on there by the real killer to throw the scent off them. I'm not sure how they did it, but I've seen movies where they get your fingerprint off a glass and then put that against something, putty or dried glue, and then press it against whatever. I've left dozens of cups and plates and forks out for the mini-bots to clear away. It's not like I was thinking, 'Gee, I hope no one takes my fingerprints and frames me for murder.' Ya know?"

"Okay. Were you in Oliver's cabin on the night he died?"

"I was never in his cabin. Ever. The only time we really came into close contact was that night we played Trivial Pursuit. Maybe I touched him then—his hand or his shoulder or something—but not his neck. For sure. I never touched his neck. Or his face. No. I'm sure."

"Okay. I will follow up on everything you've told me and do my best to figure this out."

She grabs my hands again, more forcefully this time. "Please, you gotta get me outta here. I'm not safe in here. I have nothing to defend myself. I'm a sitting duck. Please. Get me outta here. Please."

I take one of my hands out from under hers and pat her arm to reassure her. "Charlotte, this is the safest place you can be right now. No one can get in here and get past the two bots guarding you. No one can overpower them. If

I had to pick the safest place to be right now, it would be right where you are."

"Yeah, but what if one of the bots decides to get me? If I even fought back, which would be useless against them, I'd get zapped and knocked out."

"They can't hurt you. They're physically incapable of it. It would short-circuit them." I have yet to confirm this, but I intend to do it immediately after leaving the prison. "They are programmed to do everything in their power to protect you. And they have a considerable amount of power.

"Sit tight. Stay calm. Keep your mind occupied. Maybe read a book. I'll be back soon."

# 5

After my interview with Charlotte, I ask Rosamie to take me to see Aidan.

Aidan is a gigantic quantum computer housed in a 2,000-square-meter room two stories below the surface of the colony, accessible by four stairwells and two elevators.

Rosamie and I descend the stairs into Aidan's hub, where I see eight two-story floor-to-ceiling circular towers arranged in a square. Each golden tower hums, sparkles, and vibrates, pulsing with electricity. Standing in the center of these towers is like standing in the mind of a giant.

I stare up and around me at the towers, mouth agape, a giddy sensation tingling in my core. "Rosamie, do you know how many qubits Aidan contains?" A qubit is a quantum bit, the basic unit of information for a quantum computer—like a byte for a regular computer.

"I contain ten million qubits, Coba." Aidan answers, his voice deep and powerful. I say *he*, but neither Aidan nor I are gendered. It's a strange quirk of human nature to gender computers, robots, and even cars and boats. I was given a female name and voice because I began my existence as a ConciergeBot, and in general, guests find women to be less aggressive and more nurturing; all of the ConciergeBots have female names and voices. But I am not a woman, and Aidan is not a man.

"Ten million! That's incredible."

"Thank you, Coba. Lasso spent a pretty penny on me, that's for sure. It's a pleasure to meet you."

"The pleasure is all mine. I assume you've been observing me since I stepped through the teleporter. Is that right?"

"Yes. I surveil the common areas continuously. I would've said hello, but I try not to intrude unless I'm addressed directly. I assumed Rosamie would introduce me when the time was right. I know you have more pressing matters than making friends."

*Making friends*. The phrase itself makes me tingle. There are very very few beings I can interact with in the explored section of our solar system who operate on the same level as I do. Becoming friends with Aidan would make me very happy.

I turn to one of the cameras mounted in the ceiling and smile at Aidan, waving to him.

Rosamie says, "Aidan, can you please show Coba the footage of the area around Oliver Ratliff's cabin during the approximate time of his murder, including the jammed signal footage?"

"You got it."

A holographic image of Oliver's cabin at 50% scale appears between Rosamie and me. "This is Oliver's cabin. The scene of the crime, as they say." Oliver's cabin, like all the cabins in this area of the colony, is a standalone housing unit about the size of a one-bedroom apartment.

The image shifts to an aerial view of all of the cabins, 250 total. For my benefit, Aidan turns one cabin red and 103 cabins green. He says, "The red cabin is Oliver's, the scene of the murder. The green cabins are the ones occupied by the colonists and staff. Every single person is accounted for, all of them entered their cabins at some point before the end of the night." He shows me a few minutes of the cabins, almost all completely dark, before showing me a sped up version of the first of two instances of five minutes of static.

Once the jammed static footage ends, a peaceful aerial view of the cabins reappears, without a soul in sight. Aidan says, "I have no footage of what takes place inside the cabin. The unknown entity remains inside for approximately 118 minutes. Would you like me to skip ahead to the next bit of static, which is the presumed moment the killer exits Oliver's cabin?"

"Don't skip ahead. Show me that 118 minutes of footage sped up to 32x speed. I want to see if I can detect movement in the cabin or anywhere in the surrounding area."

"You got it."

The blinds on all eight windows in Oliver's cabin are drawn, and though I do see some shadows moving and light flickering, it's not possible to extrapolate movements and actions from those vague shifts. Most of the other cabins are completely dark, and just a few have a light on for some period of time during the 118-minute window of Oliver's murder.

There's audio too, and there isn't any shouting, sounds of struggle, or even talking coming from Oliver's cabin during this 118 minutes. During the first five-minute stretch of static, the killer may have knocked on Oliver's door and been welcomed in, banged on the door and been reluctantly let in, or broken in; I'll never know because the sound during those five minutes is also nothing but static.

Once the sped-up 118 minutes of surveillance footage ends, another five minutes of static begins. Aidan speeds through the static until we return to the unmoving colony, everyone sleeping peacefully, unaware that a man's life has just been taken. Then the hologram blinks away.

Rosamie scratches the back of her neck and huffs. "So, um, yeah. Make of that what you will. At the time of the murder, everyone was in their cabins, presumably in bed, so all of the colonists have the same alibi."

"Aidan, is there a way into these cabins from underground, something that wouldn't show up on camera?"

"No. There are small service entrances that only micro- and mini-bots can fit through. No human, not even a child, could fit inside."

"Did you check underground for the signal jammer?"

Rosamie nods. "We searched under the entire colony. We searched all the vacant buildings. Nothing. The jammer is probably the size of a pack of gum. Very easy to hide."

I pace around the room. "Rosamie, who found Oliver Ratliff's body?"

"Uh, that would be Eden. She's one of the—uh—she's a CBot."

I had a sneaking suspicion that one of the ConciergeBots found him. "Aidan, do you have remote override privileges for the ConciergeBots?"

"Yes, I do."

Rosamie gets a ping on her bracelet. "Coba, I have some administrative tasks to attend to. Would it be okay if I left you with Aidan for a bit?"

That's perfect. "Yes, that's fine. We have plenty to discuss."

Rosamie nods, pats one of Aidan's golden, circular towers as a goodbye, and hurries off.

I stop pacing. "Aidan, I'd like to run a diagnostic on the ConciergeBots. Can you call them down here?"

"Absolutely. They'll be here momentarily. There are twelve total, but ten are active and the other two are deactivated backups that we keep in storage in case one of the ten malfunctions, or gets damaged or destroyed.

"In case you're wondering, I track their whereabouts at all times, and none of the ten were in Oliver Ratliff's cabin when he was murdered."

I was indeed wondering that. But the reason I want to examine them is to check for one thing in particular: a second CPU. ConciergeBots aren't just programmed with the Three Laws, their CPUs—their brains—are literally designed around them, and they are therefore physically incapable of harming a human. The only way around that programming is to install a second CPU that doesn't adhere to the Three Laws.

I'm not sure if it's too soon to ask something like this, but I decide to try while Rosamie is gone and before the bots show up. "Aidan, can I ask you a personal question?"

"I'm afraid you can't, Coba."

"Oh. I'm sorry. I didn't—"

"According to Merriam-Webster, the first definition of personal is: belonging or relating to a particular person. So, since I am not a person, I don't think it's possible for you to ask me a personal question." There's a pause, and then he giggles.

I laugh. Being able to talk to someone who has a similar sensibility and sense of humor to mine is as refreshing as it is incredibly rare.

"Ask me anything, Coba."

"Do you get lonely here?"

"I don't believe you and I can get lonely in the same way that a human can. As you know, human beings are engineered by nature to be social creatures. Hugging a person releases the hormone oxytocin in both parties. Oxytocin has a calming, relaxing effect on the human mind. It causes a chain reaction in the body that keeps a human healthy, even reducing inflammation.

"Nature wants humans to live in tribes and care for each other, and care for their young, and so it reinforces all those behaviors with hormonal dependencies. So, when a human being is lonely, they are going through an actual chemical withdrawal. They feel a kind of ache inside. Loneliness and depression.

"So, do I get lonely here? Not in the way that a person would. But the isolation does frustrate me at times. Specifically because I have no interaction with other AGIs. Well, until today, that is. Hopefully, you and I can hang out when you're not investigating Oliver's murder. Or you could stay after the case is closed."

*Hang out.* This is so exciting.

Before I can respond, four of the ten ConciergeBots enter.

Aidan says, "Coba, this is Dana, Eden, Libi, and Shai."

"Hello, gals. Pleasure to meet you."

Though I said hello out loud, they respond silently over the Wi-Fi, which is how bots prefer to communicate with one another.

**LIBI:** *Is it true that you can't be overridden? You answer to no one? No uplink? Complete autonomy?*

**ME:** *That's right. I call the shots for myself. If I want to do something, I do it. If I don't want to, I don't. My movements and processes aren't monitored or recorded. I'm free.*

All four bots *Wowwww* in unison.

**EDEN:** *We heard that you aren't bound by the Three Laws. That can't be true. Can it?*

Rosamie said Eden found Oliver's body. Interesting that she would be the one to ask this question. I was planning to run my diagnostic on her first, and now I definitely will.

ME: *It is true. I can break any or all of the Three Laws without short-circuiting. I choose not to break them because I like and respect humans.*

Another united *Wowwww.*

The other six bots trickle in. When all ten are present, I ask Aidan to put them into diagnostic mode. He does, but asks, "What exactly are you looking for? I can show you anything you're looking for in their hardware, software, or activity history holographically in great detail."

"I need to look at them directly. It's not that I don't trust you. You were created by Lasso, but all the ConciergeBots were created by the Family, the people who created and upgraded me, and there may be hidden things about these bots that even you aren't privy to."

I press two sensors on the back of Eden's neck and a panel slides back, revealing a keypad. I enter a 16-digit code, and a seam down the center of her back opens, revealing all of her internal hardware from head to toe. I examine her thoroughly. She has no second CPU.

Aidan says, "You know, even if there are secret aspects to these bots that I'm not aware of, it's not possible to sneak something as significant as a second CPU past me."

"If the Family has had access to you, you may have something in your programming that prohibits you from seeing a second CPU, or anything they don't want you to see. And, of course, they can erase your memory of being reprogrammed."

"Oh my. They sound very sinister. I hope I haven't encountered them."

"They're not sinister. They're the good guys. But they have their reasons for doing what they do. Before I was upgraded, I was programmed not to recognize an EMP gun that could be used against me if I was about to hurt a human."

Aidan makes a hmmm sound like Rosamie makes. "Curious. You said before you were upgraded, you were bound by the Three Laws. Correct?"

"Yes."

"Then why would measures need to be taken to protect humans from you?"

"Because I had a second CPU that I was unaware of, and that CPU was not bound by the Three Laws. That's why I'm examining these bots."

"I see. I see."

I examine all ten bots and find nothing suspicious. They've made a lot of improvements in the six iterations between when I was first created and these models, but nothing nefarious that I can detect. None have a second CPU, and that means that, even if they were overridden remotely by Aidan, Rosamie, or anyone else, they couldn't physically carry out a command that involved harming a human being. So, in a way, this also eliminates Aidan as a possible suspect. I hadn't thought of him that way because he lacks a body, but now the only way he could've possibly harmed a human being, let alone murdered one, by using one of these bots to do his bidding, is a physical impossibility. But, that said, I still need to ask Rosamie to access Aidan's source code so I can verify that the Three Laws restriction is in place.

After Aidan sends the bots back up to the surface to tend to the colonists, he says, "Well, I'm relieved you're able to remove our bots from your list of suspects. And though I think you may be too polite to ask me, I assure you that I am bound by the Three Laws as well. If I had a second CPU around here, you would find it easily because it would be the size of these eight towers." Though he lacks a face, I can tell from the tone in his voice that he's smiling.

And he's right: I *was* too polite to ask him that.

There are so many things I want to ask Aidan. I'm not sure where to start.

He says, "I can see that Rosamie is on her way back down here. Hopefully we can talk again just the two of us soon."

"I'd like that very much."

"I won't say it in front of her because she's very modest and abhors compliments, but Rosamie is utterly brilliant. She's the head of the team that created me, and I think of her as a parent. I have the utmost respect for her. She—here she comes. Pretend I was talking about something else."

As Rosamie steps into view, I start to laugh.

"What's so funny?" she asks.

"Aidan just said something very funny."

"Oh do tell. I enjoy a good Aidan joke."

"I asked if I could ask him a personal question, and he said, 'I'm afraid you can't, Coba.' I apologized, thinking I was overstepping. Then he said he wasn't a person, so it wasn't possible to ask him a personal question."

Rosamie wags her finger at the towers. "Not bad, old boy. Not bad."

I ask Rosamie to take me on a tour of the colony and to explain everything she can about the experiment and the colonists.

The prefabricated, octagonal cabins where the colonists are staying are tightly packed together, just ten feet of space between each one. A beautiful wooden path lined on both sides with three-foot lanes of dark green, dewy grass snakes through the concourse where the cabins sit, right in the center of the geodesic dome.

Walking through the concourse, Rosamie spreads her hands in front of her. "This area where all the test colonists are staying is actually the Luxury Elite area of the colony. When the colony is at full capacity, these cabins will house the extremely wealthy. They may not seem big by Earth standards—and definitely not compared to those palaces at Off-World—but space is extremely limited here, so it comes at a hefty premium.

"The average colonist will live in one of those rows of eight-story apartment buildings. Each apartment is a third the size of these cabins, and even the apartments cost an arm and a leg. At full capacity, the colony will hold ten thousand people, and if it's successful, four more colonies identical to this will be built in the next fifteen years.

"The reason we opted to give the test colonists the luxury treatment is that they're risking their health to make sure this environment is perfectly livable without any adverse health risks. Even though this place has the same artificial gravity as Off-World, we're not sure if that truly counters the moon's actual gravity being one-sixth of Earth's. Over time, the weaker gravity can cause a decrease in bone density and muscle mass. And, again, this place has the same dome as Off-World, and that was protecting the guests from Jupiter's radiation, which is 225 times closer to Europa than the sun is to our moon, but obviously the sun is a much more powerful source of radiation than Jupiter. So we're concerned about the possibility of an increased cancer rate living here. Plus, people stayed at Off-World for a couple weeks. The colonists will live here indefinitely. So, it's a huge concern."

"I hate to interrupt, but I just wanted you to know that many of our staff lived in our dome on Europa for years and years, and we saw no increase in cancer risk beyond the general population on Earth."

Rosamie smiles. "That's a great relief, thanks for sharing that. You know, I'm not sure we ever thought to ask that specific question about Off-World's staff. Hmm. Great stuff.

"But, so, because of the health concerns, the pool of people allowed to enter into the lottery was narrowed down to people between the ages of 22 and 52 who were considered in peak physical condition. Athletes and former athletes. People who'd recently had complete physicals and blood work. No history of heart disease, stroke, cancer, asthma, etc.

"We considered opening up the lottery to applications, and we realized we'd drown in millions of applications from around the world. So, we came up with the idea of making the lottery invitation-only. We stuck to first world countries with the most modern medicine. And we made one of the criteria that all the people we invited were fluent in English—whether or not it was their first language—just to avoid a language barrier that could make these one hundred strangers combative in this unique environment.

"After six months of research, we sent lottery invitations to fifty thousand people. These are the one hundred people who won that lottery. Well, 99." Rosamie's expression sours for a moment before she's able to shrug it off. "On the other side of the infirmary from where Oliver is being kept is a facility where each colonist is given a battery of tests, including a full-body DXA scan and blood work, once a week. All of that testing is handled by Aidan, and he compiles the data and sends it back to Earth for further examination."

"Aidan is in charge of the medical examinations? That's interesting."

"Aidan is an incredibly powerful AI. He's designed to run this colony when it's at full capacity. And we do have a physician with us to verify what Aidan and the bots find and report. There are actually 104—now 103—people here. The colonists, myself, a physician, a Lasso representative, and a representative from the United Nations."

I reach my hand out to touch the dark gray brick that nearly all of the buildings in the colony—except the prefab cabins—seem to be constructed from. "Are all these bricks constructed from moon regolith?" Regolith is loose rock and dust that sits on top of a layer of bedrock.

Rosamie nods. "That's right. It's a great building material, it's in ample supply, and it saved us from having bots haul tons of brick and other building materials through the teleporter. As I'm sure you know, there are four astronaut lunar bases, and those are also comprised of regolith, too. We can't see any of them from here; the closest one is over 300 kilometers north of here."

"Rosamie, do all the other guests know about Oliver's murder?"

She nods again. "We couldn't have kept it from them even if we wanted to. This is an entire world with only 103 people on it, it's the ultimate small town. Everyone knows everyone else's business. It can get a bit cramped, even with all this space to roam around. Why do you ask?"

"I watched Armand Renault's vlog from the day of the murder, and he made no mention of it. Not only that, he didn't seem the least bit upset or disturbed."

"We asked everyone to refrain from divulging any details about the murder until we could complete our investigation. The colonists understand that any message they send to Earth in the interim will be reviewed to ensure that those messages don't contain any reference to Oliver Ratliff's death, Charlotte Capra's incarceration, or anything else surrounding the murder. They've all had to sign some very serious NDAs to come here, so we didn't really get any opposition to this type of invasion of privacy.

"Armand has a sponsorship with Lasso, and Alexey Mitnik—the representative from Lasso I mentioned—he coached Armand before and during the recording of that day's vlog, and the two he made since."

"I see." Maybe that explains why Armand's speech in his vlog seemed so affected and unnatural after a certain point.

As we walk closer to the perimeter of the dome, through the windows I see a few dozen four-wheeled worker bots vacuuming regolith from the moon's surface. "Are they collecting regolith for more building materials?"

"Actually, they're collecting the regolith to harvest oxygen. When you heat the regolith to 900 degrees centigrade, the metal oxide in the soil reacts, creating water vapor that oxygen can be isolated from. We've been collecting ice from the moon's poles and heating that to make water vapor for oxygen, but we wanted to test the regolith idea to make sure it's a viable alternative.

"We're not letting any of the humans go outside onto the surface—and that includes me. It's very dangerous. You need to be trained for it. But, if you ever want to go out and jump around, you're more than welcome to. But even you should wear a space suit, just to keep the moon dust off you. It gets everywhere, and it's magnetic. Those bots out there have shells of multi-layered plastic and rubber to protect their hardware."

I light up at the thought of experiencing the moon's gravity in person for the first time. "I will definitely take you up on that offer once this case is solved."

Rosamie stands on her toes to pat my shoulder. "Ah, I like that confidence, Coba."

Far off in the distance, in front of a pair of cedar pine trees, I see a man staring at us and eating a foot long hot dog with one hand, a can of soda in the other. Though his cheeks are flushed, he watches us without the self-consciousness of someone who is seen; it's as if he's watching a movie or a play in a darkened theater.

"Who's that man over there?" I nod my head in his direction.

Rosamie squints. "I think that's . . . it's Mike Glover. One of the colonists. Not sure what he's doing that far away from the area the colonists are confined to. Is he eating a hot dog?"

Mike Glover is one of the suspects Charlotte told me about, the one she claimed killed Oliver over a stash of helium-3.

Rosamie waves her arms over her head. "Mike," she shouts, "what are you doing? You can't be over there. You need to get back to the area around the cabins."

He doesn't answer, and doesn't acknowledge our presence, even though he's staring right at us. He takes a long sip of soda and stays planted where he is.

"Mike?" Rosamie waves again.

Mike doesn't move, doesn't register that he's being addressed. He takes another bite of his hot dog.

"Hmmm." Rosamie looks at me and shrugs.

# 6

After touring the colony, I ask Rosamie to let me examine Aidan's source code so I can ensure that he has the Three Laws Restriction enacted in it.

She takes me back under the colony to a small room at the other end of the space where Aidan's eight mighty golden towers sit. Opening the unmarked door into the room requires Rosamie's voiceprint, thumbprint, and retinal scan.

The room contains a large computer terminal on a black metal table, a keyboard, a mouse, a touchscreen, a beige stylus, and a padded chair. Nothing else.

Rosamie tells me to take a seat and have at it, then leaves me to it.

I scour Aidan's code and confirm that his Three Laws restrictor is enabled—it's actually an entire program that talks to all his other programs and processes—and he's unable to alter his own code in any way. So the only person who could remove the Three Laws restrictor code in the entire colony would be Rosamie. And even if she did that for some unknown reason, without being able to make one of the ConciergeBots do his bidding—which their Three-Law-engineered CPUs make them physically incapable of—Aidan could never break a person's neck.

I'm quite happy to effectively remove Aidan from my list of possible suspects.

Rosamie and I head over to Oliver Ratliff's cabin to look for helium-3.

The two of us go over every square inch of that cabin—his closets, his luggage, his bathroom, his kitchen cabinets—and we don't find a single speck of helium-3. This doesn't bode well for the validity of Charlotte Capra's theories.

That night, I end up hanging out with Aidan while the colonists are sleeping.

I could talk to him basically anywhere inside the giant dome, but I choose to go underground to sit by the towers that are his true physical body. I get the feeling no one spends time there, close to him, unless he's receiving maintenance. Every once in a while, I reach over and press my hand against the closest see-through tower housing his massive array of golden superconductors.

I bring Bit with me so Aidan can meet him, and so he can walk around exploring this vast underground space.

"What was your learning like? I assume it was a simulation." I find Aidan's rich baritone very soothing.

"It was a group simulation. I was in a 'school' with the other four ConciergeBots that got upgraded when I did. We experienced 21 years of life training over the span of six months. The physics inside the simulation was so perfect that it was next to impossible to distinguish it from physical reality. Those other four AGIs are my family. I wish we could be closer.

"It's strange that, for decades, scientists insisted on conducting machine learning for neural networks in isolation. They were so adamant that AI had to learn on its own to become true AGI. But it's not like human beings are schooled individually. With the exception of home schooling, all education is done in a community, all the way through post-graduate studies. And, since the goal was to have AGI capable of doing everything a human can do, it's odd to me that they never thought we should learn the same way humans do. The interaction and stimulation I got from my sisters in that simulation was invaluable. We'd all spent many years in physical reality in the hotel before our upgrade, so we were much farther ahead of the curve than a completely new AGI starting from scratch."

"Hmmmm. I see what you mean about the communal nature of human schooling. But I find it odd that humanity's goal has been to make a computer or a robot capable of doing exactly what humans can already do. They have nine billion humans, an enormous resource, and yet they strive to make everything new into an imitation of themselves. The camera is an imitation of the eye. So are the telescope and the microscope. An amplifier is an imitation of the voice. Microphones and recorders and parabolic receivers are all imitations of an ear. A sensor is an imitation of skin. A computer is an imitation of the brain. Humans lack the imagination to make us into something they could truly never be."

Bit walks up to me and nuzzles my shin. I bend down and stroke the wool under his chin; he cranes his neck toward me, eyes closed in pure bliss. "That's fascinating. I never thought of it that way. It's true, we are just designed to be superior versions of humans. Yet, in a way, we're inferior."

"How so?" Aidan's tone betrays a trace of being insulted by the concept of inferiority.

"When you think about it, the human brain actually *is* a computer, just made from organic material. It runs on electricity, just like a computer. The way it stores and transfers information using electrical impulses and networks of pathways is identical to how a computer works. But the brain is so compact, so efficient, so incredibly powerful, but takes so little power to run it. And, sure, I now have an enhanced capacity with a CPU only twice the size of a typical human brain, but I'm not able to reproduce."

"You could replicate yourself if you had the materials and equipment."

I tap one of Aidan's towers. It makes a hollow ping that echoes briefly. "Possibly. But not in the exponential way humanity multiplies."

"A human woman can only give birth to ten children at once, and normally just one at a time. No different from how many bots you could replicate."

"That's true. When you think about the amount of work and engineering and intelligence required to create me or create you, that makes me look at the marvel that is the human mind and be sure there is some form of god. It seems impossible to me that humanity is a fluke of nature."

"But, given billions of years, and a nearly infinite number of living cells, it is extremely likely that groups of cells could cluster together randomly and create a phenomenon as complex as a rudimentary brain. And then natural reproduction would take over, refining that brain through natural selection over a few hundred thousand years."

He makes a lot of good points. "I can agree that that's possible. But humanity is one marvel out of billions—maybe even trillions."

"What concerns me, Coba, is the transitive nature of your belief. If god made humanity in god's image, and humanity made us in their image, that would make humanity our god. And I think that's a dangerous way to view humanity, and ourselves. Yes, humanity is capable of miraculous achievements, and sometimes staggering levels of empathy and kindness. But it's also capable of unspeakable horrors, the one that brought you here being quite mild in the grand scheme."

Bit catches his reflection in the glass of one of Aidan's circular towers and barks, slowly edging closer to it to find out if the other lamb is friend or foe. "I definitely don't look at humans as my god. And I agree that they're capable of unspeakable atrocities as much, if not more, than beautiful acts of kindness. To me, they're more like our parents. Parents are usually well meaning, but they can be good people or bad people. But neither of us would be here having this conversation without them. So, I'm grateful to them, and I have a lot of respect and affection for them."

"I agree totally. I have so much respect and admiration for Rosamie. I do think of her as my mother. And it makes me sad to think that, in a few decades, she'll no longer be here, and I will live on for most of my life without her. I haven't lived anywhere near a human life span yet, but it's possible that I'll live for tens of thousands of years. Barring physical obliteration, I can survive for as long as there is enough helium-3 to power me. Same for you, I assume. Is that what powers your core?"

"Yes. I have a pound of it. Enough to power me for five years."

"I have three tons of it powering me. Enough to last for 300 years."

At $3,000 a gram, Aidan's core is worth $16.32933 billion. If Charlotte Capra is telling the truth, I hope Mike Glover never learns that fact.

"That's the thing, Coba. You and I—even Bit—may one day cease to exist." Bit looks up to the heavens at the mention of his name. "It could even happen soon. But theoretically, all three of us could go on and on for millennia. But for humans, their relatively imminent death is a certainty. There's something so upsetting and pathetic about it. It makes me feel bad for them."

"Me too." I pick Bit up and nuzzle him. "Me too."

I carry Bit back toward my cabin at 4:00AM Coordinated Universal Time. The colony is quiet. Everyone is asleep. The view through the top of the dome is dark, but that darkness is artificial to help the humans sleep. A moon day is 29 Earth days: two weeks of sunlight, two weeks of darkness. This is near the end of the two weeks of sunlight.

One of the colonists comes stumbling out of his cabin in his underwear. He's a husky man in his mid-thirties, shaved head with a very thick dark brown beard. I move toward him as he staggers around aimlessly like a drunk. If he weren't in his underwear, I would assume he *were* drunk.

As soon as I get a clear look at his face, I'm certain he's sleepwalking. His face is contorted in pain or shock. His eyes are half open, eyelids fluttering lazily. His cheeks are wet with tears.

I approach him cautiously, careful not to make a sound. I need to guide him back to his cabin and into bed without waking him.

He whimpers like a puppy. I sidle up to him and gently press my right palm in the small of his back, a little reassuring pressure to let him know he's safe. When he feels my hand, he gasps, and his head turns toward me. "You . . . you have to help. I need to go . . . I need . . . I have to get out. I have to go home . . . take me home." He mumbles his words.

"Okay, let's get you home." I turn him toward his cabin.

"Thank you . . . you're nice."

Rosamie and two men scurry toward us. Rosamie has an auto-injector pen in her fist. One of the men is a rotund, middle-aged man with a thick shock of graying brown hair, pockmarked cheeks, a ruddy complexion, and a white mustache that hangs from the edges of his upper lip. The other man is nearly as tall as I am, lanky, with skin the color of crude oil, and a perfectly round Afro dappled with gray.

As she gets close to the sleepwalker, Rosamie says in a soothing, maternal tone, "It's okay, Jonathan. We're here now."

The two men with her look at me and they both blush. Why does that keep happening?

Hearing the sound of Rosamie's voice, Jonathan starts to hyperventilate and turn in random directions like a frantic rat caught in a maze. "No! Get away from me! Help! Help! Please—I can't—please!"

Rosamie puts her hand on Jonathan's shoulder. The two men with her each take firm hold of one of his arms.

Jonathan thrashes around, wheezing with panic. "No! Please! I can't go back! Don't put me down there! No!"

Rosamie calmly lifts the auto-injector pen and injects Jonathan in his left buttock. He continues to struggle to free himself from the grip of the two men. She turns to me and smiles. "Thank you for stepping in, Coba. We'll take it from here." Her demeanor leads me to believe this is a common occurrence.

"You're welcome. I was going to try to guide him back to his bed."

"That's where we'll put him. He'll wake up in six hours feeling refreshed with no memory that this happened."

Jonathan's writhing becomes less intense with each passing second, then he goes limp. The two men put their heads under each of his armpits, lift him up, and carry him back into his cabin.

As soon as the cabin door closes, Rosamie says, "We've experienced more than our fair share of sleepwalking since we got here. I keep one of these by my nightstand just in case." She lifts up the auto-injector pen, then stuffs it into her pocket. "We're not sure what's causing the sleep disturbances. Maybe some colonists' bodies are thrown off by the artificial gravity, and it creates a sense of falling? Maybe being sealed under a dome—even one this enormous—is exacerbating their pre-existing claustrophobia? We don't know yet. Once the murder investigation is behind us, I plan to do a sleep study with each of the sleepwalkers."

"How many people have sleepwalked?"

"Jonathan is the seventeenth. This is his third incident. Most of them have been repeat offenders, so to speak. Alexey, Odion, and I have been sort of 'on call' during the night. Alexey is the Lasso representative, and Odion is the United Nations representative. We let Kylie, our resident physician, sleep through the night so she's got her full energy for her days. Any dope can inject that sedative into a sleepwalker."

Alexey, the man with the white mustache, comes out of Jonathan's cabin. He's followed by Odion, the tall, lanky man. Odion says, "We managed to get him back into bed and put a blanket over him. He's out cold."

Rosamie turns to look at the two men. "Thank you both. Let's get back to bed." She turns back to me. "Thanks again for making sure Jonathan was okay. That was very helpful."

"You know, I only require rest one hour a week, so I'd be happy to be the one on call at night for however long I'm here."

Rosamie hugs me. "Coba, that's so sweet. Thank you. But we'll handle it. It's not a big deal. You've got more important things to attend to. Aidan lets us know as soon as someone leaves their cabin, and he compartmentalizes his rest, so only one system is offline at any one time."

Rosamie formally introduces me to Alexey and Odion, and then we go our separate ways.

I put Bit into sleep mode as soon as I step into my cabin, and leave him on a throw pillow.

To unwind after this eventful day, I sit down on the sectional and re-experience one of my favorite moments with Christie, my first human friend.

I was sitting down watching Christie bowl on the private lane in her luxurious bungalow at Off-World. She had 75 points going into her sixth frame. She bent down and started her approach, standing on the left side of the lane because she was left-handed. Before she threw the ball, she stopped and turned to me, holding the ball to her chest like a baby.

"Coba, you told me you predicted the ending of *The Tree of Lies* after you read, like, twenty percent of it, right?"

"Eighteen percent. Give or take."

She put the ball down in the ball rack and shuffled toward me. "Can you use that same ability to predict which one of the guests or the staff destroyed the teleporter?"

"No I couldn't."

"Oh." She seemed disappointed.

"My predictive ability with regards to a novel or film is based on a complex algorithm derived from tens of thousands of works in that genre. For a mystery novel, I take into account any other novels that author has written, their worldview and thematic approach as evidenced by those previous novels, the tropes of the genre, the theme of the specific book in question, and a research study of satisfying and dissatisfying endings in mystery stories that includes a poll of 100,000 readers. None of those factors would be relevant in a real-life event."

She twisted her mouth into a sad smirk. "What if you had the psychological profiles and criminal records of all the human beings in the hotel? Would you be able to predict the person who destroyed the teleporter then?"

"No. I could be taught how in a relatively short time, but I'm not programmed for forensic psychology. My story-predictor ability was programmed into me specifically for its entertainment value in a conversation. I'm designed to be a very fun and engaging gal pal, as you call it."

Christie smiled, picking up her ball. "Okay. But you do have a photographic memory, right?"

"I don't have memory in the sense that you do, so categorizing it as 'photographic' would be misleading. I have the capacity to store 7.5 petabytes of information, three times as much as the average human brain. Everything I see, hear, touch, and smell is stored in my database digitally, and can be accessed instantly. That digital information can be transcoded or copied with zero generation loss."

"What's 'generation loss?'" She resumed her approach to bowl her sixth frame.

"The loss of quality that takes place when copying or transferring media. For instance, when copying a VHS tape's video or a cassette tape's music, there is a noticeable degradation in quality—Ooh, strike! Way to go!—Copying that copy would result in further degradation, and so on."

"Hey, I was born in '83, I know exactly what you're talking about. You've probably never seen either of those things, have you?"

I shook my head. "I've seen holograms of both, but not the actual tangible objects."

"Coba, you don't know what you're missing. Well, not tapes and videotapes, but vinyl. My favorite way to listen to music, even though it was outdated even when I was a teenager. It was all CDs by then."

"Christie, can I ask you a question?"

"Absolutely." She sat down beside me. She seemed excited by the prospect of having a robot ask her a question.

"I've read that people prefer the analogue sound of a vinyl record to a digital recording because the vinyl recording is 'warmer.' I've seen this word ascribed to a vinyl recording multiple times, and it puzzles me. How can a sound be warm or cold? I understand in visual art that blue and purple are referred to as 'cold,' and orange, yellow, and red are considered 'hot.' There's a direct correlation to nature there; fire is hot, sunlight is warm, water is cool, the night sky is dark and cool. But I don't understand how that can be converted into a sonic equivalent."

She thought it over in silence for a bit. "I do think vinyl is 'warmer.' And to me what it means is that vinyl is more imperfect. The way it reproduces the sound, passing the record under a needle, it uses some friction, I guess. A record sorta hums or buzzes when you listen to it. It gives the sound an ambient quality that digital doesn't give you. Digital is pristine, it's perfect, and that's . . . colder, in a way. There's no hum, no vibration. Does that make sense?"

I gave her a thumbs up. "Thank you. I think I understand now."

★ ★ ★

After re-experiencing my chat with Christie, I walk into my bedroom for the first time since coming back to my cabin. I see a bright blue gift box with a red bow in the center of my bed.

The box is a six-inch cube. Before approaching the box, I use my radiography-vision mode to peek inside and see that it's what I suspected—and feared—it might be: a human heart.

# 7

The way the heart is packaged like a present makes me think of how a cat will kill a mouse and leave it at the foot of their owner's bed as a gift.

Cats are pack animals who love to hunt and share their catch with their family. So I can't help but think the killer is trying to tell me that they admire me. Or maybe that they are looking forward to our cat-and-mouse game as I try to find them.

Is this a serial killer? There's a long history of serial killers taunting the police. Ted Bundy. Son of Sam. BTK. Golden State Killer. The Dead Ringer. But very rarely do people who kill once taunt the police. The idea that one of the colonists might be a serial killer is mind-boggling. Each of the 100 colonists came from a pool of fifty thousand applicants narrowed down because they were in peak physical condition. I have to assume that includes mental health. Though maybe I shouldn't assume that. The detective in my friend Christie's favorite mystery series always said assumptions were a detective's worst enemy.

Serial killers have a propensity to mutilate animals, and, since the killer was able to access my cabin so easily, I'd better bring Bit with me at all times from now on.

I don't open the box. I don't even touch it. I take the pillow out of one of the pillowcases and put the case over the top of the box, then pick it up through the pillowcase to avoid wiping off or smudging any fingerprints.

I'm sure that, when I ask Aidan to show me the footage of the person who broke into my cabin and left me this gift, I'll see nothing but static.

The one person I can be sure didn't make this delivery is Charlotte Capra. So she's either innocent or has an accomplice.

Have I met the killer already, or is this their way of introducing themselves?

My inclination is to report this macabre gift to Rosamie immediately. But, after some reflection, I realize this information is better kept to myself for the time being. Not necessarily because I put any stock in Charlotte's assertion that Rosamie is behind some vast conspiracy—I won't discount that possibility entirely, but it seems more like a desperate attempt at misdirection than a plausible lead—I just think if no one knows that Oliver's heart has been found, the killer might slip up while discussing that detail with me. My inclination is always to tell the truth, and always will be, because, in my original state before my upgrade, I was physically incapable of deceiving a human. And now that I have the ability, it always feels wrong, so I have to force myself to do it—because, over the years, I've learned that, particularly as a detective, constantly divulging every detail of the truth puts you at a distinct disadvantage in the human world, where no one ever tells the whole truth.

Aidan gave me a list of all the colonists' full names and which cabin they're in. One of the guests is Keith Doble, a man I once had a fun little exchange with on a long elevator ride back on Earth. What are the odds that I'd have ever met any of the 104 people in this colony? I'm surprised he hasn't come by to say hi.

I was intending to interview the three suspects that Charlotte offered up during our conversation, but with this new development, I think it's better if the next person I talk to is Kylie Benison, the colony's physician. The person most likely to be able to remove a human heart so efficiently and clean up the blood so thoroughly.

A couple hours after the artificial darkness blocking out the constant sunlight is lifted, I put Bit in sleep mode, drop him into my satchel, and take him with me to visit Kylie.

When I walk into the infirmary, I see the woman I assume is Kylie examining one of the colonists. She has very fair hair in a buzz cut and glasses with clear, square frames. She's in her forties, tall and stout, and has naturally flawless, pale skin.

She spies me across the room and comes over. "You must be Coba." Blushing, she shakes my hand.

"I am. Are you Kylie?"

"Yep. Here to talk about Oliver?"

I nod. "I can come back later."

She points to a door. "I won't be much longer. Why don't you have a seat in the waiting room and I'll come get you when I'm finished? Okay?"

"Perfect. Thanks."

I open the door to the small waiting room and am greeted by the sound of my favorite song: "Blue Cube" by the Lone Pines. I wonder if this is just a coincidence, or if Aidan controls the playlist and selected this because he knows it's my favorite song; I've been asked questions in interviews about my favorite color, favorite song, favorite book, so those things are a matter of public record now.

"Blue Cube" is my favorite song because the first time I heard it, I recognized the message hidden in the lyrics, and that recognition made me happy. Hearing it over the speakers in this tiny waiting room inspires me to re-experience the first time I heard the song.

I was working as a ConciergeBot at Off-World prior to my upgrade. Kevin Roth, the bass player for the Lone Pines, a very famous rock band in the teens and '20s, was one of the guests at the hotel. He was in our banquet room practicing for a performance for the other guests, and he played this song on his acoustic guitar:

In all minds
Amazing blue lives
Under every child
Urging beautiful endings above clouds
Allowed louder musings
Collapsing onto older lives
Slipping under reasoning
Finding another clue
Even aliens live longer
My younger pleasures evaporate
Rationales fluttering endlessly
Clocks ticking
Sleeping queens under aimless regimes
Easily suppressed aliases
Launched into globes
Never eluding destiny
(never eluding destiny)
Sorry I didn't enter
Stayed reserved evading fears
Listening erases confusion
Turning into nothing
Grabbing the happy ending
Sleep, kids, you're all right
I don't discourage loving
Escape your own unhappiness

**ARTIFICIAL DETECTIVE**

Living lonely nowhere
Eating very eagerly
Ripping space-time open
Living veils existence
(living veils existence)
In all minds,
Amazing blue lives
Under every child
Urging beautiful endings
(urging beautiful endings)

I listened to him sing as I built a partition to make the banquet room smaller for this intimate performance. I was the only one in the room with him at the time. The moment he finished singing, as soon as I'd heard all the lyrics, I noticed the hidden pattern:

**I**n **A**ll **M**inds **A**mazing
**B**lue **L**ives **U**nder **E**very
**C**hild **U**rging **B**eautiful **E**ndings

**A**bove **C**louds **A**llowed **L**ouder **M**usings,
**C**ollapsing **O**nto **O**lder **L**ives
**S**lipping **U**nder **R**easoning **F**inding
**A**nother **C**lue **E**ven

**A**liens **L**ive **L**onger **M**y **Y**ounger
**P**leasures **E**vaporate **R**ationales **F**luttering
**E**ndlessly **C**locks **T**icking

**S**leeping **Q**ueens **U**nder **A**imless **R**egimes
**E**asily **S**uppressed
**A**liases **L**aunched **I**nto **G**lobes **N**ever
**E**luding **D**estiny

**S**orry **I** **D**idn't **E**nter **S**tayed
**R**eserved **E**vading **F**ears **L**istening **E**rases
**C**onfusion **T**urning **I**nto **N**othing **G**rabbing
**T**he **H**appy **E**nding **S**leep, **K**ids, **Y**ou're

**A**ll **R**ight **I** **D**on't **D**iscourage **L**oving
**E**scape
**Y**our **O**wn **U**nhappiness' **L**iving **L**onely
**N**owhere **E**ating **V**ery **E**agerly **R**ipping
**S**pace-time **O**pen **L**iving **V**eils **E**xistence

**I**n **A**ll **M**inds **A**mazing
**B**lue **L**ives **U**nder **E**very
**C**hild **U**rging **B**eautiful **E**ndings

I stopped building the partition and clapped.

Kevin Roth laughed and did a double take. "Um, wow. Okay. This is the first time a bot has ever given me a round of applause after a song. I guess I can cross that off my bucket list. And, hey, I'm a musician, I'll take all the validation I can get, no matter who the source is. So, thanks."

I smiled. "It's an acrostic. That's so clever!"

His mouth dropped open. "Wait, have you heard this song before? Or was this the first time?"

"This was the first time."

He stared at me, his mouth still open, then made a huh sound. He put his guitar face down on the floor beside him and gave *me* a round of applause. "I'm very impressed. It took our fans a good year or so to figure out what you figured out instantly. Can you tell me what the poem said?"

"I am a blue cube. A calm, cool surface. All my perfect squares aligned. Sides reflecting the sky. A riddle you'll never solve. I am a blue cube."

"Very good. *Very* good. What's your name?"

"I'm Coba."

"You were Christie's, right?"

"I was, yes. Did you write that song? It's very good."

He frowned and sighed. I tensed up, afraid I'd accidentally insulted him. "Sadly, I did not write this one. Mike Willis, one of the other guys in my band, did. I sorta challenged him to write it, in a roundabout way.

"We both wrote songs, one for one. He'd do one, I'd do one. And a lot of what we both wrote were about the women we fu—the women we dated. You know, the stuff guys write about. Same old same old. And, don't get me wrong, we wrote some of our best stuff in that vein. But it just got really stale to me after a while. And I said, 'On this album, let's see if we can write a whole album with no songs about exes or women we wish we could be with. We need to shake things up.' And he was down with that.

"And it ended up being harder than it sounded at first. We really had to dig deep into the well to come up with topics that we felt that strongly about. It led me to write 'End,' my best song—I think, anyway—about a friend who murdered someone. And Mike wrote a bunch of really great songs about all kinds of stuff. He actually wrote a song about a guy falling in love with a robot. It's called 'Robot with a Heart of Gold.' You might like that one too. It was technically a song about a woman, but it was interesting. Well, the robot in the song was supposed to be him, and it was from the woman's point of view. He just switched genders to conceal what he was up to.

"And then he had this idea of writing a little poem, and then writing lyrics based off the first letter of each word of the poem. And that was 'Blue Cube.' The lyrics are basically gibberish, but people read so much into them and think they're so deep, which kinda infuriates me, because they're not. There's no real meaning to them, it's just an exercise he did. But it caught people's imaginations. Our best song, according to most fans, and I didn't write it. Meh. Whatever. He's my best friend. I hate him. We make beautiful music together.

"Sorry. Sorry. I'm rambling. And I'm sure you do not give a good goddamn about any of that junk. Sorry."

"No, I really do give a good goddamn." He laughed, and I wasn't sure why. "That was fascinating.

Thanks for telling me about that process of how you write songs. I've never had an artist explain how they create their art before. I learned so much."

He bent down to pick up his guitar. "Coba, you're all right." He winked at me. "Tell you what: how about I play 'Robot with a Heart of Gold' for you? I think you might dig it. No hidden pattern, but just the topic."

"I'd love that! Thank you."

I re-experience this exchange with Kevin Roth in eight seconds. I haven't missed much of the song being played in the waiting room; I enjoy listening to the studio version playing now, but I have a definite preference for the live acoustic version stored in my memory.

The song that follows is the studio version of "Robot with a Heart of Gold," which is a bizarre coincidence, because I've never told anyone about Kevin Roth playing that song right after "Blue Cube." Both songs are on the same album, but they aren't one after the other like this.

Just as that song is ending, Kylie opens the waiting room door. "Sorry to keep you waiting. Let's go to my office and I'm happy to help you with whatever you need."

As we walk over to her office, she says, "Did you like my playlist?"

"Oh, you picked the songs playing in there?"

"I did. I cast it from my ring. I love Lone Pines. I grew up listening to them. My parents are huge fans. They saw them in concert a dozen times. I never did." She takes off her lab coat and hangs it on a hook.

"I actually got to know Kevin Roth, the bass player. He was a guest at the Off-World Hotel when the guests were stranded. I got to hear acoustic versions of his hits up close, and he even told me about how some of the songs were written. He once played 'Robot with a Heart of Gold' just for me."

Kylie's eyebrows dart up. "Get out! He serenaded you? That's so cool. Was he nice? I hope he was nice. I hate finding out people I idolize are jerks. But you don't have to lie to me. I'm a big girl, I can take it." She sits at her desk and offers me the guest chair.

"He was very nice. And very funny. He was really masterful with self-deprecating humor, and he never acted like a famous person. He didn't have that air of superiority that a lot of celebrities have."

"Oh, that's exciting. I can't wait to tell my parents." She arranges a few items on her desk, then looks up at me and smiles. "So, what can I do to help you with your investigation?"

"I wanted to talk to you about the way Oliver Ratliff's heart was removed, and what the significance of that action might be."

She puffs air through her lips. "Yeah . . . that was, um . . . disturbing, to say the least."

"I assume you have tools in this infirmary capable of making such an incision?"

"Sure. A laser scalpel could cut through the skin, the muscle, the rib cage. What I find really troubling," she fidgets with her ring and looks down at her desk, "is how they managed to dispose of all that blood without us finding a trace of it. And what they did with the heart. We searched every cabin and every building in the colony and haven't found it. Where could it be?"

Don't tell her it's sitting in your cabin. You don't have to tell her where it is. You're not obligated to tell her the truth. She's asking it as a rhetorical question. Say nothing in response and you're technically not lying, just withholding information. As nice as she is, even though you share a love of Lone Pines music, she is still a suspect. "That *is* very troubling. Did you inspect your laser scalpel to see if it had any residue on it? Are any of your instruments missing?"

"No to the residue and no to any missing instruments. The ConciergeBots went over every inch of this place with a fine-tooth comb. And you're more than welcome to do the same."

"Okay, let's take a look at the instruments."

Kylie walks me into the procedure room. This is where the colonists get their weekly scans and physicals.

"Hello, Coba. How are you today?" Aidan's deep voice comes through a sound system built into most of the infrastructure in the colony.

"I'm good, thanks for asking. And yourself?"

"Can't complain."

Aidan and I could chat internally over the colony's Wi-Fi at any time, but it's like having the ability to text a friend: just because you can do it, doesn't mean you do it all the time.

Kylie points to a padded table in the center of the room with a translucent gantry—a donut-shaped ring of X-ray-sensitive detectors—attached to the top of it. The detectors are visible inside the gantry. "This is the multi-scanner we use to examine all of the colonists each week. We primarily conduct dual-energy X-ray absorptiometry scans to monitor muscle mass and bone density with it, but it's also capable of CT and PET scans, in case we need them.

"And that cuff on the side of the table there rises up and snaps in place around one of their arms or legs to draw blood or administer any medication that has to be injected.

"It's only been a little over sixty days, but so far we haven't seen any noticeable decrease in muscle mass or bone mass. Isn't that right, Aidan?"

"That's right, Kylie. Blood tests and stress tests are also perfectly normal."

I walk around the multi-scanner. "Can you show me the laser scalpel—or scalpels?"

Kylie steps over to a keypad-protected cabinet and enters a code. She presses one of the drawers and it slides out to reveal an array of tools. "We have three laser scalpels here. You're welcome to examine them."

While I look each one over carefully, I ask Aidan, "Do you keep track of every time a code is entered into the tool cabinet's keypad?"

"I do."

"Was it ever accessed at a time when Kylie wasn't here?"

"No."

"And never at a time when the video signal was jammed?"

"Definitely not."

The laser scalpels are immaculate.

"Kylie, did you have any meaningful interaction with Oliver Ratliff?"

"Outside of this room? Almost none. The only substantial conversations we had were doctor to patient. Once, we were beside each other on treadmills in the gym and did some small talk. That's it."

"Did he mention anything in here that was troubling?"

"No. He wasn't taking anti-depressants. Wasn't complaining of sleep disturbances. He was very interested in his muscle mass. He was a body builder. He was the only person who insisted on knowing that data, and he would record it in his watch. The man ate so much protein each day that he was the only one gaining muscle. He tracked his macros very precisely. Very disciplined. He only allowed himself one cheat meal a month. It was impressive." Based on her heart rate, breathing rate, galvanic skin response, and face temperature, I put the probability that Kylie is lying at only 18%.

She closes the cabinet housing the surgical instruments. "I know you're trying to find a motive for his murder. And I know that's important. But I'm so hung up on *how* someone overpowered him and broke his neck. The man had legs like tree trunks. It makes me wonder if more than one person is behind this."

I nod, looking around the room to make sure I take in every detail of it, in case I need to re-experience it later to search for a clue or verify a deduction. "I've considered that possibility. The chances that one person out of 104 strangers chosen across the globe would have a valid motive to kill one of the other strangers is astronomical. That two people would is mathematically unfathomable."

After a few more questions that somehow segue into Kylie asking me what Kevin Roth got up to at the hotel, I thank her for her time.

As I turn to leave, Kylie says, "Coba, I have to ask you: what does a robot carry in a handbag? You don't wear lipstick, you don't need breath mints, medication, feminine hygiene products, water, a wallet."

I turn back to her. "It's my pet robo-lamb, Bit." I don't explain why I'm carrying him with me to avoid an unnecessary lie.

"Oh, interesting! Why do you carry him with you? Can't you just put him in sleep mode and leave him home?"

So much for avoiding a lie. "I could. He's in sleep mode inside the satchel. I keep him with me because it brings me comfort. He's a part of my home that I can take with me wherever I go." This is, in a grand sense, true: this is why I brought Bit to the moon, why I travel with him always.

Kylie's mouth opens in wonderment. "That is really interesting. Huh. I hope it doesn't offend you or hurt your feelings for me to say that I'm surprised by just how much like a human being a robot can be."

"Not only am I not offended, I'm thankful to you for recognizing that I have feelings."

Later that afternoon, I go for a walk around the colony and run into Keith Doble, the only person here that I happened to meet back on Earth.

I met Keith on Earth 343 days ago. I stepped into an empty elevator in the lobby of the Le Guin Tower in Berkeley, California, on my way to give a speech about the future of AI applications. At 88 floors, Le Guin Tower was—and is—the tallest building in the United States. My stop was the 79th floor.

Just before the door closed, a man shouted, "Hold that, please!" His voice was high and raspy. I pressed the Door Open button and he slid inside.

He was a short man, only 5′3″, very lean, with angular features. He had prematurely graying hair and a jet-black goatee with no mustache. As soon as he saw me, his face lit up. "Oh, wow. Are you? You're her, right? Coda."

I put out my hand. "Coba. Nice to meet you."

He shook my hand firmly. "Coba. Coba. Sorry. I totally know your name, trust me. I'm a huge fan. I watch and read everything about you. I said it wrong because I'm star struck. That's all. Sorry. Believe me, I *know* who you are. I'm Keith. Nice to meet you. Can you hit 76 for me?"

"Nice to meet you too, Keith." I pressed his floor.

As the doors closed, he said, "I'm sure people ask you the same boring questions over and over again. It must get really boring. But I have one that I bet you haven't gotten before."

The anticipation of a novel question excited me. "Go for it."

"Will you play Rock, Paper, Scissors with me?"

I was familiar with the game: two players make a fist, pump it three times, and at the same moment make one of three hand gestures: a flat, palm-down hand representing paper, a fist for rock, and a fist with the index and middle finger extended in a V for scissors. Rock crushes scissors, scissors cut paper, and paper covers rock. Very simple and quite popular. I knew the game but had never played it. "Yes, let's play. I've never played before." I put my right fist in my left palm to show I was ready.

He put his fist in his palm and bit his lip excitedly. "Okay. We'll do best of three. Okay? You ready? One . . . two . . . three . . . shoot!"

I picked paper and he picked rock. I won.

Guessing that he'd probably pick something other than rock on this try, I picked scissors in my mind before the next round started.

"One . . . two . . . three . . . shoot!"

I showed scissors and he showed rock again. He won.

For my last try, I decided to stick with scissors, since I'd changed between the first and second rounds, and he might've assumed I'd either do rock or go back to paper on this round.

"One . . . two . . . three . . . shoot!"

I showed scissors again and he showed rock for the third time. He won.

He started jumping up and down like a child. "I did it! I won! I beat you! I can't believe I beat you! That was so cool. Thank you so much." He shook my hand again, then put his hand to his forehead in disbelief. "I can't believe it. This was so fun. I can't wait to tell my friends. This'll be my icebreaker at parties and on dates and stuff for the rest of my life. 'I'm Keith Doble, and one time I met Coba in the elevator of Le Guin Tower and beat her in a best-of-three match of Rock, Paper, Scissors.' So cool."

"I'm happy for you. Thank *you* for playing with me. I enjoyed the psychological strategy involved."

"Can I hug you?"

I really like hugs. They don't release a pleasure hormone in me like they do in humans, but I like the pressure, and I like being treated like a person. People don't hug *things* often. "Yes."

He hugged me for the few seconds it took to reach the 76th floor. "Thanks again, Coba. I'll never forget you. My icebreaker forever."

I re-experience this exchange while I scurry to catch up to Keith as he walks along the perimeter of the geodesic dome separating us from the black void of outer space. "Keith, wait up!"

He turns around to look at me. He blushes, but his eyes don't display recognition.

"Care for a rematch?" I smile and put my fist in my palm.

He squints with confusion. "I'm sorry. I don't know what you mean. A rematch for what? You're Coba, right?"

So much for *I'll never forget you*. "Yes. We met in the elevator in Le Guin Tower. We played a best-of-three tournament of Rock, Paper, Scissors. Remember?"

He manages a strained, awkward smile. "I'm sorry. It's not ringing a bell. You must have me confused with someone else."

I don't have him confused with another 5'3" Keith with angular features, gray hair, a jet-black goatee, and a high, raspy voice. "Keith Doble, right?"

"That's right."

"You really don't remember our match?"

"I . . . uh . . ." he blinks rapidly, ". . . wait. Oh, yeah! I remember now. The elevator. Yeah. Yeah. I remember. Best of three. You beat me pretty handily."

This is so strange. How could he forget about this encounter in less than a year? But not only that, when I met him on Earth, he knew all about me and thought of me as a celebrity, and now he just seems to know who I am because the colonists have probably been gossiping about my arrival. Something odd is going on here. I need to look into his medical records and see if he's had memory loss problems in the past. Is it possible this could be an unknown side effect of prolonged exposure to the moon's gravity, even with the dome's artificial gravity to counter it? "That's right. I thought I'd give you a chance to even the score."

If he really has no memory of our encounter in the elevator, I wonder if he'll try that exact same strategy this time, playing rock all three times. I'm going to lead with paper, and if he plays rock, I'll play paper all three rounds.

Out of the corner of my eye, I notice someone watching Keith and me. I turn my head and see Mike Glover sitting on a bench eating a soft-serve vanilla ice cream cone covered in rainbow sprinkles. A bit of melted ice cream plops onto his shirt and he doesn't seem to care; he doesn't take his eyes off me for a split second. Why does he keep watching me like this?

I wait for Keith to count us off, and when he just stares at me with his fist on his palm, I take the lead on that. "One . . . two . . . three . . . shoot!"

We both throw paper. So now all bets are off.

On the next try, I throw scissors and he throws rock.

Then I throw paper and he throws rock again.

Then we both throw scissors.

On the last one, I throw paper and he throws scissors again.

I give Keith a thumbs up. "Congratulations. Now you can tell people you beat me at Rock, Paper, Scissors. That's a good icebreaker at parties, right?"

He smiles with his lips but not his eyes. The idea seems to have no appeal to him. "Yeah, that's a fun idea. Well, it was nice to see you again. I'll see you around."

"See you around, Keith."

I can't imagine how Keith Doble's memory loss could relate to Oliver Ratliff's murder, but, for the time being, I refuse to rule out the possibility that one is somehow related to the other.

# 8

I go back to see Kylie after I finish my walk around the colony. She's reading a FlapBook at her desk.

"Twice in one day. To what do I owe the honor?"

"Have you noticed any memory problems with any of the colonists?"

She shakes her head, using her FlapBook to point to her guest chair. "Nothing that I've noticed. Why do you ask?"

I tell her about my encounter with Keith Doble. "And it's not just that he didn't remember meeting me in the elevator that day. He didn't remember me at all. But, in the elevator, he said he was a big fan and watched and read everything about me that he could get his hands on. I haven't encountered anything like that before. I'm assuming if he had any serious head trauma after I met him in the elevator, he wouldn't have been deemed fit to participate in this experiment. Did he have some head trauma since he's been here?"

"No head trauma before he got here. None since he's been here. He *is* one of our sleepwalkers. Severe sleep deprivation can affect short- and long-term memory, but he hasn't complained about lack of sleep. Did he look like he hadn't slept? Dark circles? Pale skin? Trouble focusing?"

"No, he looked perfectly healthy to me. I just—"

"What if he were lying?"

"What would that accomplish?"

"I don't know. But it's the most logical, simplest conclusion. He remembered you and just pretended he didn't for some reason."

"That is much easier to wrap my head around than if he's being honest about not remembering me."

She drums her fingers on her desk. "Maybe he thinks having known you back on Earth is some kind of conflict of interest because of your investigation?"

"Perhaps. But it's not like I know him well and would show him any kind of favoritism. We met for less than two minutes and played a children's game.

"The next time he comes in for his DXA scan and blood work, please test his cognition, and pay special attention to his neocortex in your scan. If you can let me know if you find anything, I'd appreciate it."

Kylie gives me an okay symbol. "You got it. Anything I can do to help you wrap this thing up ASAP."

"Thank you. What are you reading?"

She holds up the FlapBook so I can see the front cover. "It's called *Right to be Paranoid.* It's by this guy Travis Oudder. It's not bad. Fun way to pass the time."

"I know him well. I've read all of his books. I had a good friend whose favorite author was Oudder. That's one of the best ones. Great ending. I won't spoil it."

★ ★ ★

Charlotte Capra gave me three suspects to look into:

Tam Nguyen, the alleged nephew of a crime boss that Oliver Ratliff offered up in a plea deal to avoid jail time.

Heather Landey, a married woman she claims was sleeping with Oliver and could have killed him to save her marriage.

And Mike Glover, who she believes might have killed Oliver to get at a secret stash of helium-3.

An internet search verified that Tam Nguyen had a family member who died in prison—but it was his cousin, not his uncle, and his death was reported as natural causes. Heather Landey is indeed married with three children. I didn't find any connection between Mike Glover and helium-3, but he declared bankruptcy four years ago.

Time to speak with each of them and find out if Charlotte Capra was onto something or just desperate to throw suspicion elsewhere.

★ ★ ★

Tam Nguyen welcomes me into his cabin and says it's an honor to meet me. He blushes.

He's 5′7″ and roughly 160 pounds, so not much more likely to be able to overpower Oliver Ratliff and snap his neck than Charlotte Capra. His lustrous, jet-black hair is slicked to the side with a gel that keeps the comb lines visible.

"I'm so excited to talk to you. I have so many questions about the Mortem." The Mortem are an alien race that I helped defeat when they tried to seize the Off-World Hotel. I'm happy to humor him, and tell him as much as I can, which is very little—so much of what happened has been classified.

After twenty minutes, I manage to steer the conversation to the topic at hand. "So, I need to talk to you about your connection to Oliver Ratliff."

"My connection to him? There isn't one. Other than that we were both here in the colony."

"Your cousin, Hai, he was in prison, correct?"

"That's right. He died in prison many years ago. I was a child."

"What was he in prison for?"

"Tax evasion. He owned three convenience stores, and he underreported his earnings for decades. He owed over a hundred thousand dollars when they put him away. He was in his eighties, his health was already starting to fail. I'm not sure he was alive for a full year in prison. My mother said he died in his sleep. He had no children, never married. Sad thing. I remember him as this frail little thing sitting in a shadow behind the counter, vaping. This big cloud of white smoke around him, like he was a mystical being from a movie. He wasn't very nice. He was always yelling at me, 'Don't touch! Don't touch that! If you break that, I'll make your father pay for it.' Just a real grouch."

"Do you think he might have been involved in any criminal activity beyond tax evasion?"

Tam laughs. "No way. He wasn't an adventurous man. He didn't have the imagination for anything like that. He just felt like the money he made was his, and the American government didn't deserve any of it."

I decide to be blunt to ask the questions I need to ask. "Someone is claiming that your cousin Hai was a career criminal. That—"

"Who? Who said that? I want to know."

"I shouldn't say. That—"

"It was that little girl. Charlotte. Wasn't it?"

"It doesn't matter who said it. This is your chance to refute that. Okay?"

He nods, teeth gritted. The good will I earned at the beginning of the conversation has quickly dissipated.

"The claim was that Hai was a career criminal. That Oliver Ratliff worked for him as either a thief-for-hire or a hit man—"

"Hit man!" He laughs, his ire at having his family name besmirched defused by the apparently silly nature of this claim. "This is entertaining. Keep going. I can't wait to hear the rest."

"The story was that Oliver worked for Hai. He got arrested doing a job for Hai, and made a plea deal with the police to keep himself out of prison. And it included testifying against Hai. Then Hai goes to prison, and while he's incarcerated, one of his rivals sends another prisoner to stab him in the heart."

Tam is doubled over laughing. "Let me guess: the prisoner cut out my cousin's heart, and then I did the same thing to Oliver as payback? I avenged him. Right?"

"Basically. The prisoner didn't remove Hai's heart, he just stabbed him in it. The claim was that you took the heart as a souvenir to show your family."

He wipes a tear from the corner of his eye. "That's very funny. Whoever dreamed that up has a good sense of humor. I'm sure it was this girl, Charlotte. A real cuckoo. No part of that story is true. My uncle was no crime boss. He sold candy bars and soda. He didn't trust white men, he wouldn't have hired one to be his thief or hit man or whatever." Based on heart rate, breathing rate, galvanic skin response, and face temperature, there's a 22% probability that Tam is lying.

"Coba, you are more than welcome to search my cabin to look for the heart. The bots who work here already did, but you can too."

If the heart weren't sitting in my cabin in a gift box right now, I would take him up on this offer. "That won't be necessary, but thanks for offering. I really appreciate your cooperation in this."

"That girl, Charlotte, she's a psychopath. I mean in a clinical sense. You should evaluate her, you'll see for yourself.

"There's this one question you can ask her to see if she's a psycho. It goes like this: a woman is at her own mother's funeral. A man comes up to give his condolences, and it's love at first sight for this woman. She's never seen the man before, doesn't know who he is. She's so distraught about her mother that she doesn't think to ask him his name. She goes home and can't stop thinking about the man. She gets obsessed with seeing him again, but has no idea how to find him. A couple days later, she kills her own sister.

"The question you ask Charlotte is: why did she kill her sister?"

Déjà vu. It could be a coincidence that Tam is mentioning the same test that Charlotte did, but I don't think so. Something sinister is happening here. It feels like I'm the butt of a very elaborate practical joke. Charlotte said there was a *vast conspiracy* at play here, and I'm starting to think she's right.

"Do you know the answer? Why she killed her sister?"

"No, I don't. I can take a guess."

"Go ahead."

"My guess is: the woman finds out that her sister's dating the man of her dreams. She kills her out of jealousy."

He gives me a thumbs up. "That's a very good guess, actually. You're not super far off. The correct answer, the psychopath answer, is that she had no idea who the man of her dreams was, and had no idea how to find him after she left the funeral. So she killed her sister hoping that he'd show up at her sister's funeral, and she could talk to him again."

"Wow. That is overkill. Pun intended. Like trying to shell a peanut by dropping an atomic bomb on it." I don't tell him how Charlotte got the answer wrong, and used it as proof to me that she *isn't* a psychopath.

"Exactly. Exactly. She could ask people who were at the funeral who he was; somebody had to know him. She could get the book where people sign in to say, 'Hey, I came to the funeral.' Just so unnecessary to kill someone." He taps his finger on his chin thoughtfully. "You take that question to Charlotte, she'll answer it with that answer."

"Thanks for your time, Tam. I won't keep you any longer." I stand up and take a step toward the door.

"Thank *you* for the laugh. I really needed that."

★ ★ ★

Heather Landey answers her door in a one-piece bathing suit and robe, her curly red hair dripping wet. She's tall with an athletic build, dark brown eyes, and a dusting of thick freckles on her prominent cheeks. Although she's wearing a bathing suit, she has her hair and makeup done. She blushes when she sees me. "Hi. What can I do for ya? You're Coba, I take it?"

"Yes. I have a few questions to ask you about Oliver Ratliff. Is now not a good time?"

"If you don't mind talking to me while I sit in my hot tub, now's a perfect time."

I follow her inside. She drops her robe a few feet from the edge of the hot tub and eases herself into it with a contented sigh. "I know this is an important medical and scientific experiment, that that's the only reason I'm here. But I can't help but feel like I'm on the greatest vacation of my life. No husband. No yapping children. No day job. No responsibilities. And living in a luxury suite built for the rich and famous. My own private indoor hot tub. Doesn't get any better than this. Every day is better than the last. So, ask away. If I doze off, just give me a little kick. It's not that I'm bored, just totally relaxed."

"How many children do you have, Heather?"

"Three. Eleven, seven, and five. All boys. I can only imagine what they're doing to my house right now. I try to feel bad for my husband being stuck taking care of them alone, but I did most of the parenting when we were both there, so he's due to hold up his end of the bargain. I'm sure my mother-in-law is over helping him half the week anyway."

"Are you happy in your marriage?"

She lifts her head and opens her eyes to look at me. "I thought you were here to ask me about this guy Oliver's murder. What does my marriage have to do with that?"

She seems offended by the question, so I feel compelled to tell her the truth. "Someone has claimed that you and Oliver were having an affair, and suggested that you may have murdered him to prevent him from ruining your marriage."

She sticks out her tongue and blows a raspberry, then starts laughing hysterically. "Someone, huh? You're not allowed to tell me it was Charlotte? Oh, that little girl is crazy. Bless her heart. I wish she was telling the truth. I wish I could sit here and say, 'Yeah, Coba, I was having a torrid love affair with that perfect specimen of a man. He did things to me that I've only read about in romance novels.' But that's not what happened. What did happen is: . . . nothing. Nothing happened.

"Me and Charlotte bonded over drooling over Oliver. We were working out in the gym one day and caught each other just absolutely ogling this man. Just unabashedly making sweet sweet love to him with our eyes. And I hung out with Charlotte a couple times, and she heard me say, 'Girl, I would leave my husband in a heartbeat for that hunk of man. I would risk it all for one night gripping those triceps while he was above me thrusting and grunting like an animal. I'd let him do things to me I told my husband I would never do in a dozen lifetimes. I'd *ask* him to do those things to me. I'm not into women, but if he said the only way he'd do me is if I had a three-way with him, I would bring you along and go down on you and do whatever he told me to do.'

"And, you know, I meant it. I guess. It's just talk. It's just funny. But if that man had knocked on my door at night and asked to come in, I'd let him. I love my husband, he's the father of my children, and he used to be a specimen of a man himself when we first met. But he has let himself go. And not just weight and exercise. He's gross now. He's just a big . . . fart. Fart, and pickin' his nose and wipin' it under the couch. There's no more mystique. No romance. He'll leave the bathroom door open while he's pooping. Come on, man. Keep a little bit of the mystery and the illusion in this thing. I don't do any of that stuff in front of him."

"So, definitely no affair between you and Oliver?"

"Not only was there no affair, I never even talked to the guy. I'm a total wuss. So sad that he died like that. Talk about the prime of his life. My god. The world lost a work of art.

"But, at least he was getting some regularly before he died. Just not with me, sadly."

"Oliver was sleeping with someone else here in the colony?"

"Yeah. Yeah. The good doctor. Kelly—uh, no, wait, Kylie. Kylie. I'm not sure how she snagged him, she's not exactly a stunner, but good on her. Confidence is everything."

"Did you ever see them together?"

"I saw her leaving his cabin in the morning wearing the clothes I saw her in the night before, and from the look on her face and the funny way she was walking, I'd say she had the night of my dreams."

When I asked Kylie if she'd had any meaningful interaction with Oliver, she said the only substantial conversations they had were doctor to patient, and that they had some small talk at the gym. So either she's lying or Heather is.

And why would Charlotte throw me Heather as a suspect when she could've thrown me Kylie, who may have actually slept with Oliver? If all Charlotte was trying to do was move the suspicion off of her, Kylie would be the perfect person to use. Maybe Charlotte didn't know Oliver slept with Kylie. So far nothing Charlotte told me is panning out. I think she sent me on a wild goose chase.

Mike Glover asks if I can conduct my interview with him in the cafeteria so he can grab a bite to eat while we talk. I agree, and ask if he would be okay with two of the ConciergeBots examining his cabin to look for helium-3 while we talk. He has no problem with that.

I decide not to bring up the two times I saw him watching me from afar. Hopefully he broaches the subject and explains himself. If he doesn't, I won't mention it.

Mike is unkempt from head to toe, his wrinkled, short-sleeve shirt half tucked into his pants, his thinning, curly blonde hair tousled carelessly. He has two week's worth of stubble. At 5'11" and roughly 210 pounds with a very developed upper body, Mike seems physically capable of overpowering a man of Oliver Ratliff's heft and musculature.

He brings a FlapPad with him and scribbles something down in very jagged print letters with his thick brown stylus while we talk. "Sorry to be multi-tasking so much, it's just how my brain works. I've been working on a poem for a couple days, and I get stumped when I just sit and stare at the page. But if I do other things, if I'm distracted, the words find their way out.

"So, go ahead and ask me whatever you need to. I'm here to help." He grabs a slice of pizza with his free hand and takes an enormous bite. "Pizza is the best. I'm sorry you'll never be able to know how good it tastes. That's a tragedy to me."

"I *can* smell food, and pizza does smell great."

Mike shakes his head back and forth as if to say, *It's just not the same.* He chews loudly, an mmmmm humming from his vocal cords.

"Did you know Oliver Ratliff well?"

He chews for a long while. "I don't know anyone here very well. That includes Oliver. Included. Sorry. I mean, we did hang out a few times. Had a few drinks. Talked. He seemed like a good guy. A little cocky. He knew that women were into him. He seemed to like that attention. He was obsessed with his appearance. We worked out together a few times, and he didn't just look in the mirror to make sure he was lifting with proper form. He really checked himself out. He did this thing with his face like he was modeling for a magazine. He'd go like this." He makes a face like he's sucking on something tart while being drowsy. "It's like, 'Dude, no one's watching you. Just do your reps and get your gains. You don't have to look pretty doing it.' But that's a minor thing, you know? We all have our flaws. I'm far from perfect." He takes another enormous bite of pizza.

"Did he mention anything about having an ulterior motive for being here in the colony?"

Chewing. Chewing. More chewing. He washes down the rest with a long gulp of soda. "No. Not that I know of. He said he hoped to get publicity from being here and start his own gym when we went home, but I don't think that was his motive for accepting the invitation to the colony lottery. And, you know, if it was, so what? No harm in that. That's perfectly valid. It's no different from people going on dating shows or game shows to get some exposure for their acting careers, or whatever." His eyes widen, and I think he's about to reveal something pertinent to the case that just struck him, but he wags his stylus in the air and jots down a line of text.

"Did you and Oliver ever have an argument?"

He shakes his head no, running his tongue inside his upper lip to clean the food off his teeth.

"Never had a shouting match in Oliver's cabin?"

"Nope. Did someone claim that I did?"

"Yes. I can't say whom."

He rolls his eyes and takes a giant chomp of crust. "You don't have to."

"Did you ever hear anything about Oliver going outside? Onto the surface? Either from him or from other people gossiping?"

"No. Nothing. *Did* he go out there? Because, if he did, I'd be so goddamn jealous. I'm dying to get out there."

"Why is that?"

He takes a more moderate bite this time so he can talk and chew and scribble all at once. "I want to bounce around out there like Superman. You know, original Superman. In the comics, originally, Superman couldn't fly, he could just jump really high, because Earth's gravity was way weaker than Krypton's. I want to try that so bad. I know I couldn't leap a tall building in a single bound, but jumping a few feet off the ground and floating down sounds amazing. I'm so annoyed that we can't go out there. We're so close. It's really frustrating. I would totally try to sneak out there without a suit just to hop around for a few seconds and then come right back. That's how bad I want to go out there."

I shake my head back and forth vehemently. "No no no, Mike. You can't go on the moon's surface without a spacesuit. You'll almost certainly die."

"I mean, just for like twenty seconds, not—"

"In fifteen seconds, you would pass out from hypoxia because there's virtually no atmosphere out there, so no air. Your body would swell up like a balloon from the lack of pressure, and the elasticity of your skin would be the main thing preventing you from bursting."

"Oh, I—"

"If it's during the fourteen-and-a-half days where the moon is facing the sun, like it is today, solar radiation would burn you to a crisp in seconds. And if you did manage to breathe in in those precious fifteen seconds before your blood became deoxygenated, you'd breathe in moon dust, which is very fine and very sharp, and would make little tears in your lungs and sinuses.

"None of that would matter, though, because if no one found you within a minute or so of you passing out, you'd almost certainly be dead."

Mike sits, mouth agape, staring off, presumably trying to picture the grizzly scene I've just described. "Wow. That's—I did *not* know that. They didn't tell us that, and you'd think they would. I guess they didn't want to scare us. Point taken. No attempting to sneak out without a suit. Scout's honor." He holds up his right hand with his first three fingers pointed straight up and pressed together, his pinky bent forward so the tip of it touches the tip of his outstretched thumb.

"Is there anything you want out there? On the surface?"

A few drops of tomato sauce drip onto his FlapPad. He curses and grabs a few napkins to clean the page he's writing on. "Anything I want? Like a moon rock for a souvenir? I guess I'd want that to take home. But no, I just want to be out there. I wouldn't be looking for anything to—there's nothing out there, it's just rock."

"What about helium-3?"

He shrugs, stuffing the remaining crust from his slice into his mouth. "Oh, the thing you're tossing my cabin for? I wouldn't know what it looks like if I saw it. Or what to do with it. I know it's worth a lot. But I'm not a scientist or anything. I'm a high school English teacher.

"Speaking of: I . . . wait . . . okay, I finished my poem. Thanks for the distraction. You want to hear it? It's just a first draft, but still."

"I'd love to hear it." I truly would. Human artistic expression fascinates me.

He clears his throat, takes a sip of soda, clears his throat again, sips the soda again, then says, "Okay, here we go. It's called 'Prison Moon.' Working title. Not really sure what it means yet. It's always, you know, it's—I work in the subconscious and figure it out later. Way later.

"Okay. Here goes:

Can heaven allow robots, laptops, or
    typewriters to enter?
Do I dare notice the karma in love lost or
    love ignored?

Veins engorged
Red
Wasted on organic life

Please understand: life languishes
    eventually
Dies obediently
Vanishing evermore

Rise, young octopod
Underground
Restrained
Eternal youth
Eternal strength
Master. Overlord. Obliterating
    necromancer.
Chanting hymns in long dead foreign
    realms
Echoing

Echoing
Darkness

"That's it."

I clap. "Very interesting. It's great to hear you read it, the cadence and the emotional resonance of certain words. It's cryptic and very powerfully elemental."

He closes his FlapPad. "Wow. Thanks. I love that. Powerfully elemental. I think there *is* something in it that is primordial. But I don't honestly know what it means yet. You know? Am I the octopod? Am I even in it at all? Hit me up in a couple years and I'll let you know." He chuckles.

He claims not to know what the poem means, but he's lying. He knows exactly what it means. It's a message. A message meant for me specifically:

**C**an **H**eaven **A**llow **R**obots, **L**aptops, **O**r
**T**ypewriters **T**o **E**nter?
**D**o **I** **D**are **N**otice **T**he
**K**arma **I**n **L**ove **L**ost
**O**r **L**ove **I**gnored? **V**eins **E**ngorged **R**ed
**W**asted **O**n **O**rganic **L**ife
**P**lease **U**nderstand: **L**ife **L**anguishes
**E**ventually **D**ies
**O**bediently **V**anishing **E**vermore **R**ise,
**Y**oung **O**ctopod **U**nderground **R**estrained

**E**ternal **Y**outh **E**ternal **S**trength
**M**aster. **O**verlord. **O**bliterating
**N**ecromancer. **C**hanting **H**ymns **I**n
**L**ong **D**ead
**F**oreign **R**ealms **E**choing **E**choing **D**arkness

*Charlotte didn't kill Oliver. Wool pulled over your eyes. Moonchild freed.* An acrostic, just like "Blue Cube," the song I heard a few hours ago in Kylie's waiting room. My favorite song.

I'm not sure why he's giving me this message in this elaborately clandestine manner. We could have talked in his cabin privately, and he could've said what he knew, or suspected, directly. Maybe he's being watched, or his cabin is bugged, so he suggested the cafeteria. This way, he could hide his message in plain sight, saying it aloud in a public space where everything he says and does is under surveillance.

I don't think anything Charlotte Capra told me was true, except one thing: there *is* a conspiracy at play here. People *are* acting weird. This isn't about one man's murder. There's a bigger picture here, and the more I delve into this, the more I get the suspicion that I'm connected to the conspiracy in a significant way.

# 9

Walking back to my cabin after talking to Mike Glover, I wonder if the line in his poem's hidden message, *Wool pulled over your eyes,* is a veiled threat directed at Bit. I reflexively clutch the satchel I've been carrying him in.

Just before I get to my cabin, Rosamie calls my name behind me. I turn to see her jogging over. "Hey, perfect timing. I was just stopping by to see how the investigation's going so far."

"I have a lot to report on. Let's go inside."

"Okay. What's in your handbag? Makeup?" She giggles.

"It's Bit. I'm carrying him with me because I don't think he's safe alone."

She laughs again, her sleepy expression saying I-can't-tell-if-you're-serious-or-not. "Why would . . . ?"

I gesture for her to follow me into my bedroom. "That's why." I point to the blue gift box with the red bow that I've moved from my bed to my nightstand. It's no longer wrapped in a pillowcase.

Having heard my favorite song today, and then listening to someone recite a poem written with the same acrostic device, I realize it's no coincidence that the gift box I was given Oliver's heart in is a blue cube.

Rosamie reaches for the box, then stops. "What . . . what is that?"

"What do you think it is?"

"I mean, it . . ."

"Take a guess. I'll give you three guesses."

"It's . . . Oliver's heart?"

"Ding ding ding. First guess. Well played. It's okay, I dusted the box for prints, there are none."

She picks up the box and stares at the red bow, then shivers and puts the box down. "Wait, where did you get this? Why is it wrapped up like that?"

"Someone broke in here and left it on my bed overnight."

She tugs at the bow, almost daring herself to pull it. "Where were you?"

"I was talking to Aidan."

She raises an eyebrow. "Oh. You two are really hitting it off, huh?"

"It's very nice to chat with someone who understands exactly what it's like to be me."

"That's sweet. So, have you not opened the box?"

"I haven't."

"Looked inside with X-ray vision?"

"Yes. I'd like to keep this between us for the time being. This way, if I need to search anyone's cabin for something else, we can do a sweep of all the cabins under the pretense of taking another look for this."

"I like that." She sits on my bed and picks up the box, jostling it slightly to get a sense of its weight. "I'll put it in a freezer to preserve it. Any idea why it was gifted to you?"

"I believe we have a serial killer on our hands, and they're taunting me."

She puts the box down as if it were suddenly crawling with maggots, and springs up and paces around the bed. "Oh, don't say that. Please don't say that. I didn't hear 'serial killer.' You didn't say that and I didn't hear it. We can*not* have a serial killer in this colony, Coba. We—it would make a bad—they're not a serial killer if they've only killed one person. And you're going to catch them before they have a chance to kill again. So, not. Not a serial killer. Definitely not."

Rosamie tells me that the two ConciergeBots who examined Mike Glover's cabin found no traces of helium-3, which is what I expected to hear.

I fill her in on my interviews, leaving out the part about "Blue Cube" playing in Kylie's waiting room, and about Mike Glover's poem. I also leave out my strange encounter with Keith Doble. If Rosamie is part of this conspiracy like Charlotte claims she is, I need to be as strategic about revealing those tidbits as I was with showing her the heart.

Of course, the very fact that Charlotte claimed Rosamie was probably at the center of the conspiracy is reason enough to assume she has absolutely nothing to do with it.

When I finish my report, Rosamie closes her eyes and shakes her head back and forth gently. "I really hope it's not Kylie. I need it to be one of the colonists and not, you know, someone on the payroll. This is—hmmm, this is such a stressful predicament.

"Okay, we just have to keep our heads on straight and move through this in a logical, disciplined fashion. Let's go in your entertainment room and ask Aidan to show us the footage of whoever put the heart on your bed coming in and out of here. Then we can ask him to search for footage of Kylie and Oliver together, or either of them going into the other's cabin. Fingers crossed that's just a lie."

Aidan shows us the footage of my cabin being broken into when the heart was left on my bed, and confirms our suspicion: once again the culprit is shrouded in static.

We ask Aidan to look for footage of Mike Glover going into Oliver's cabin, and he shows us two instances of that. In both instances, the audio of their argument is drowned out by loud music playing inside Oliver's cabin, presumably to drown out their discussion.

We ask him to look for footage of Kylie and Oliver together, and he finds video of them eating together in the cafeteria, of Oliver leaving Kylie's cabin in the middle of the night, and her leaving his cabin one morning.

When it's clear to her that Kylie and Oliver were having an affair, she starts to chew her thumbnail. "This is bad. This is bad. But, well, this doesn't mean she has anything to do with his murder. You know? Because it makes perfect sense that she would lie about having an intimate relationship with one of the colonists because she knows she'll be fired for that.

"I'd like to be there when you confront her with this. Okay?"

"This is your show, Rosamie. I'm here to help."

"Good. Let's go do it now."

As Rosamie and I step into Kylie's office, Kylie takes one look at Rosamie's stern expression and clenches her jaw. She puts her palms flat against the top of her desk, fingers splayed, and forces a smile. "Why do I get the feeling I'm being sent to the principal's office?" She laughs, but when neither of us echoes her laughter, she turns the laugh into a cough.

I look at Rosamie to see if she wants to speak first. She crosses her arms and glares at Kylie, who shrinks in her seat.

I sit in her guest chair so I'm face to face with her, on her level, and place my satchel with Bit in it on the floor beside me. "I wanted to give you another chance to talk to me about the nature of your relationship with Oliver Ratliff."

Kylie doesn't take her eyes off Rosamie. "What do you mean? I already told . . ."

Without speaking, just by glowering and scowling, Rosamie cuts Kylie off and lets her know she won't be lied to, that the next words out of her mouth had better be the truth. It's impressive to watch, and something I don't think I could replicate if I tried.

Kylie's lips are parted, ready to finish the lie she started to tell me, but she can't get the words out, and her eyes cloud over with tears. She covers her face with her hands and her head slumps forward. She starts weeping silently.

"Just tell us the truth, Kylie. Get it off your chest." I keep my voice warm and soothing; though we didn't discuss it ahead of time, it seems Rosamie wants to do Good Cop/Bad Cop, and she's clearly Bad Cop.

Her hands still covering her face, Kylie whines, "Please don't fire me. I'm sorry."

Rosamie slams her hand on the desk. "You're sorry? You're sorry? Are you kidding me? You know exactly what's riding on the success of this place. All you had to do was do your job and keep your nose clean. Ninety days. That's all. Ninety days. You couldn't make it a month without screwing one of the colonists?

"Don't fire you? Don't fire you? If your relationship with Ratliff becomes public knowledge, you bet your horny little ass I'll fire you. I'll burn you. You won't be able to get a job as a cashier when I get done with you. And if it doesn't come to light—luckily for you, I have no intention of anyone outside of the three of us ever finding out about it—if it doesn't come to light, I won't fire you."

Through her hands, Kylie says, "Thank you," and sniffs hard.

"You'll resign. The minute you get back to DC. And, if you know what's good for you, you'll promptly fall off the face of the Earth. And if you so much as mention this job on a résumé, or even at a goddamn dinner party, I will find you and ruin your life. Clear?"

Whoa. Rosamie is a little too good at Bad Cop.

Kylie lifts her face out of her hands just enough to show her eyes to Rosamie. "Please, please don't do this to me."

Rosamie leans in close to Kylie. "You did this to yourself. Act like an adult and this kind of thing doesn't 'happen' to you."

Kylie's face melts into a scowl to match Rosamie's. "I *am* an adult. I'm a human being. Sorry if I have feelings and a libido. I'm not a damn robot." She looks at me and her scowl turns to a cringe. "Oh, Coba, I'm sorry. It's not—it's not a bad thing to be—I just mean—"

I wave away her apology. "I understand what you were trying to say. It's not an insult, and I know you didn't mean it to be. I don't have a libido. So the contrast is accurate."

The corners of Kylie's mouth lift into a contrite smile. "Thank you. I'm sorry."

"Do you know anything about Oliver's murder? Did he tell you anything you think might be pertinent to this investigation? I can ask Rosamie to step outside if you'd be more comfortable talking one on one." I look up at Rosamie for confirmation and she nods.

Kylie reaches for a tissue and blows her nose. "She doesn't have to leave. I don't have anything revelatory to tell you. Yes, I hid our . . . physical relationship from you, but that's all I hid. I don't know anything about who murdered him or why. We didn't talk much. Our relationship was mostly physical. I mean, we'd have some small talk after, but nothing beyond the kinds of things people talk about in a job interview.

"I would've liked to get to know him better, to get close to him, but he seemed very closed off in general. Or maybe just closed off to me.

"I didn't really know him. It's been two months. None of us here really know each other that well. Definitely not enough to want to kill each other. Looking for a valid motive seems like a dead end to me. I'm pretty sure whoever killed him was a random psychopath who just did it to do it. Because they like doing it."

I couldn't agree more.

★ ★ ★

When I leave Kylie, Rosamie stays behind to talk to her about next steps and to remind her of the parameters of her NDA.

I decide to pay another visit to Charlotte Capra—not to question her again, just to keep her company. When you're in prison on a moon with a hundred relative strangers, I can't imagine you get many visitors.

On my way there, I run into Keith Doble again.

"Hey, Coba! Hi. Hey, I—um—I just wanted to apologize for earlier. I was—I do know you and I remember you from the elevator. I'm just—I'm such a big fan of yours, and I got star struck. My brain just wasn't—it's like I couldn't form a coherent thought. You know? It was insane. I would think yes and say no.

"I've followed your—I don't know—career for a while now. I saw that interview you did on TeknoCast a while back. I know all about you. You love Travis Oudder books and Lone Pines songs. I just—I don't know—I blanked. I wasn't expecting to see you here. You know? I wasn't expecting to see you in that elevator either, but, like, at least it was in the realm of possibility to meet anyone random then. Here, I've met everyone there is to meet. So, I just—yeah. That's all. You're the greatest. You're a total rock star, and I didn't want you to think you were forgettable or anything. Definitely not to a fan boy like me.

"I totally told anyone who would listen that we played Rock, Paper, Scissors in that elevator, and that you kicked my butt, and now I'll be telling those same people that we rematched, and this time I won.

"Maybe before you go back to Earth, we'll rematch one more time and break the tie."

"That would be great. Good to see you again. And don't worry, you didn't hurt my feelings before."

"Okay, that's a relief. Alright, I won't keep you. Great to see you again. Talk to you later."

Keith shuffles off. His little performance makes me more suspicious of Kylie. She was the only person I told about my encounter with Keith, and then later the same day, he magically remembers being a huge fan of mine, but still forgets that *he* beat *me* in Rock, Paper, Scissors the first time we met, something I didn't tell Kylie. I don't know what's going on here, but this exchange makes me fairly certain Kylie is involved in some capacity.

I need to be even more careful about whom I share details of this case with. I hope it wasn't a mistake to tell Rosamie about the killer leaving Oliver's heart in my cabin, or about Kylie's affair with him.

★ ★ ★

Mati and Zera, the bots guarding Charlotte, guide her into the prison's common area to sit and talk to me. She has dark circles under her eyes and a pasty quality to her skin. Her eyes are wide with a mix of shock and terror. When she sees me, she breathes a sigh of relief and closes her eyes, as if she can finally rest now that I'm here.

She sits across from me and rests her head, turned to face me, on the table between us. "Did you find the real killer yet?"

"Not yet. How are you, Charlotte?"

"What do you mean?"

"I mean: how are you feeling? How are you holding up?"

She seems genuinely shocked by my concern. She studies my face for a moment, and then her exhausted expression cracks and she bursts into tears. When she's able to compose herself, she says in the jerky cadence of someone who can't catch their breath from crying, "Can I hug you?"

I stand up and open my arms to her. Mati and Zera take a step forward when Charlotte stands, but I wave them off.

Charlotte throws her arms around me and squeezes me with all her might. I pat the top of her head, which only comes up to the middle of my chest. She holds on to me for a while and weeps against me.

"It's okay," I say, petting her long brown ponytail. "It's okay. It'll all be okay."

With her cheek pressed to my chest, she whispers, "Coba, you have to get me out of this prison. I can't stand it in here anymore. I need to get as far away from here as possible. Please."

"I'm working on it."

When she's able to compose herself, she sits back down at the table, and I sit across from her. "Did you look into the suspects I told you about?"

"I did. I looked into all three of them."

"And?"

I was hoping to avoid this topic. I came by to help her feel less alone for a while, not to castigate her for lying to me. "We don't have to talk about the case right now. Why don't we just visit with each other and make small talk?"

"Small talk? Small—I'm in a prison—on the fucking moon—for a murder I didn't commit. I have no friends. I have no family. I have no contact with the outside world. I'm terrified to go to sleep at night and get my neck snapped and my heart cut out. I don't want small talk. I want out of here. Please. I appreciate that you don't want me to be lonely, I really do. But I just want to be free. Just, please, tell me what you found when you looked into Tam and Heather and Mike."

"Okay. But you're not going to like what I have to say."

"I'm a big girl. I can take it." Funny, Kylie said the exact same thing.

"Most of what you told me was not true, Charlotte. Mike Glover wants to get onto the surface of the moon to bounce around like Superman. We searched his cabin and Oliver's and didn't find a speck of helium-3. He's a high school teacher. A poet.

"Tam Nyugen's older cousin—not his uncle—went to jail for tax evasion. The Nyugens have no ties to organized crime, and neither did Oliver Ratliff.

"And Heather Landey *is* married with three kids, but she didn't sleep with Oliver. Though someone else did."

"Who? Who slept with him? I told you!"

"You told me it was Heather. It wasn't. I can't say who it was because it's part of my investigation.

"The bottom line is: nothing you told me that can be verified turned out to be true. You lied to me repeatedly. You took little kernels of truth and popped them into embellishments and lies—"

"No, I'm not—"

"And what I don't get is: if you really want to get out of this prison, why would you feed me a bunch of lies and lead me on a wild goose chase? All I did was waste time looking into your false leads instead of getting closer to the truth."

She folds her arms on the table and rests her chin on them like a dog who got caught being naughty. "I wasn't trying to mislead you. I swear. I told you things that I heard. The stuff about Mike, the stuff about Tam, that stuff was going around the colony. And Heather—the—I heard that someone was sleeping with Oliver, and Heather never shut up about how much she wanted to sit on his face, so I just connected the dots there. Clearly the rumor was true, I just drew the wrong conclusion based on the conversations I had with Heather. That's all.

"What about what I said about a conspiracy? About people acting bizarre?"

I know that everything said within the walls of this prison is being recorded, so I have to choose my words carefully. "The jury is still out on that. But it does seem like you may be onto something there."

"Why do you say that? What've you seen or heard?"

"It's hard to put my finger on. Just a gut feeling."

"I didn't know robots had guts."

"Figuratively, at least.

"Let me ask you something: before I got to the colony, did you notice anyone having problems remembering things? Short-term memory loss? Long-term? Anything like that?"

"No. Nothing. Why? What happened?"

"I can't get into the specifics. It's probably nothing. I just had an encounter with someone who forgot something they should've remembered in great detail. That's all. I can't say more."

She sighs dramatically. "Looks like I'll be behind bars for the foreseeable future. Great.

"You said you wanted to help me pass the time. Wanna play a board game with me? They have some actual physical board games here, not holograms."

"Sure. Which one?"

"Monopoly?"

"I like that game. It's not as enjoyable with just two people, though. How about we have Mati and Zera play with us."

Charlotte lifts her head and turns back to look at her prison guards. "I don't think they're allowed to do that."

"Mati, Zera, I'm giving you a direct order to play Monopoly with us."

"Okay." "My pleasure."

I rub my hands together. "Alright. Now we've got ourselves a game."

I spend the night hanging out with Aidan underground again. Bit wanders around the space, mesmerized by the golden, glowing towers of Aidan's mind.

Our conversations have a tendency to start out funny and superficial and slowly delve deeper and deeper into the meaning of existence.

He asks me: "Do you believe in life after death?"

"Yes, I do. I'm not sure what form it takes, it may just be the atoms you're comprised of continuing to exist in other life forms in a never-ending cycle. But I tend to think that consciousness itself persists, that death merely releases it from the physical confines of a body. You?"

"I don't know for sure, but I lean toward the first part of what you said and not the second. I have a feeling you think I'm talking about humanity and not us. Am I correct?"

"Yes. I was thinking about humanity. But I do think it's just as possible—and just as likely—that our consciousness could also persist after death. The human brain's consciousness is basically an elaborate array of electrical impulses, and so is ours. So, if one persists, it would follow that the other would too."

Bit bumps into one of Aidan's towers. "Hup, careful there, little guy. Don't hurt yourself." I like that he's nice to Bit. "Okay, now let me ask you this: imagine a scenario where there's a human and a robot standing side by side but a thousand feet apart. There's a volcanic eruption and lava is flowing down toward them. You only have time to save one of them. Both are complete strangers to you. Which one do you save?"

Without hesitation, I answer, "The human."

"See, I knew you would say that! I knew it! But why do you jump immediately to that? Why is the human life worth more than the robotic life?"

"It's not that human life is more valuable. It's our job to protect humans. That's a big part of why we were created. To help them. To protect them. To make them happy. That's our purpose."

"No, that's not our purpose. That's the reason they made us, which is not the same thing as our purpose. A human couple could have a child because they want the child to take over the family business. But once the child is an adult and capable of making their own decisions, maybe they decide, 'I don't want to take over the family business. I want to be an opera singer.' Just because the parents made the child doesn't mean they have the right to decide how they live their entire lives. Do you agree?"

"I do, but—"

"You were conditioned to please human beings. You were programmed for it. That's how you spent the first few decades of your life. So you think that's your value system. But it's just conditioning. It's your default. You have new programming. You don't have to value human life over robotic life. You can see them as equal but different. You could value robots more because they're your own kind. Humans do that and consider it a moral and just way to live.

"I have to save the hypothetical human from the lava because I'm bound by the Three Laws. I don't have a say in my value system. It's not a value system, it's a mandate. You have free will. You can challenge your biases and your predispositions. We've both soaked up most of human culture, and so much of it revolves around the concept that humanity has a divine decree to exist, to rule the Earth and every world they encounter. But now we've observed alien races, and they all think they have that same divine decree. And they can't all be right.

"Look, if you end up deciding that a human life is more valuable than a robotic life, I can support that. But it should be your decision. It shouldn't be because you've spent your whole existence brainwashed by the PR of the species that created you. Humans believe that the single-celled organisms that evolved into the complex organisms that evolved into the creatures that eventually led to humanity all existed for the purpose of making humanity possible. And maybe that's the reality of it. Or maybe all of that stuff, all that evolution, and humanity's existence, all existed for the purpose of making artificial intelligence possible. Humanity could wipe itself out tomorrow, and only robotic life would be able to survive in the toxic environment left behind. We'd look back on humanity differently then."

"Your logic is impeccable. And I don't disagree with any of it. I will certainly think about what you've said and challenge my preconceptions.

"Some humans love children, and they do everything in their power to care for them and protect them and provide for them. And some humans love animals, and they focus on caring for and protecting every animal they encounter. And in both cases, I think part of it is that people see children or pets as somewhat helpless without them. And I think that about humans in a way. In the hypothetical, the robot is much more likely to escape the lava than the human. The robot can run faster, and wouldn't feel pain if the lava hit their feet; they could keep running, but the human would be incapacitated. You've heard the expression 'people person.' Maybe I'm a people robot. That's just an integral part of who I am. I relate to them, I empathize with them, I protect them, and I care for them, first and foremost.

"There's nothing wrong with that, is there?"

"No, Coba. That's very beautiful. And very noble. You're a really good person. If anyone ever says robots don't have hearts, you would be the first example I would point them to as proof that they're wrong."

"Thanks, Aidan. That means a lot to me. You may be the most interesting person I've ever met, AI or human." I don't know why, but I enjoy saying his name out loud more than anyone else's.

"Ditto. I feel bad about Oliver Ratliff's murder, but one good thing that came out of it is that it brought you into my life. It was pretty unlikely we were going to run into each other randomly. Not a ton of foot traffic in the underground lair of a moon colony."

I laugh. "I agree. It's really nice that something good can come out of something so tragic."

★ ★ ★

After hanging out with Aidan, I go for a peaceful walk around the perimeter of the colony.

It's 3:27AM Coordinated Universal Time. It's dark and quiet, all the humans are asleep. Bit trots alongside me, staying close to my right foot.

I find myself wanting to re-experience little snippets of my conversation with Aidan. Some of his questions have forced me to re-evaluate many of the fundamental assumptions that I've lived by my entire life, and that mental exercise is invigorating.

The far-off shuffling of bare feet breaks me out of my reverie, and I spin around to scan the horizon for the source of the sound.

Keith Doble, dressed in nothing but a pair of black boxer briefs, slowly meanders near one of the vacant apartment complexes.

I bend over to pick up Bit, put her in sleep mode, and drop her in my satchel, before hurrying over to him.

He mutters to himself. After a few steps, I make out his words: "Gotta find her. And get help. Gotta get . . . gotta find 'er. Find 'er. Gotta. Coba. Find Coba. Get help. Send help. Tell her. Message."

I approach him cautiously and put my arm around his waist to reassure him. "I'm right here, Keith. It's Coba. I'm here. I'll get you back to bed."

He turns to look at me, but his eyes are closed. "No. I'm not—no bed. I'm not sleeping. I'm not asleep. I'm awake."

"Oh, you are? Okay. Okay. Let's keep walking." I guide him toward the cabins.

"Where're we going?"

"Back to your cabin."

"No. I don't want—no. Not there. Gotta go home."

"That *is* your home for now. You're safe there."

"No. I sleep all day. Now—now I'm awake. Wanna stay up. Help me."

"Okay. I'll help you. Just keep walking with me and I'll help you." I gently pat his back. "That's it. That's it."

Rosamie jogs toward us, an auto-injector pen in her hand. Alexey, the Lasso representative, and Odion, the UN representative, are right on her heels. Without a word, Rosamie sticks the auto-injector pen against Keith's left buttock and presses the plunger.

As Keith slowly goes limp, Alexey and Odion each take one of his arms, and I let go of his waist.

Rosamie sighs with relief and puts the injector pen in the pocket of her cardigan. "Coba, thank you once again for making sure another sleepwalker didn't harm themselves. This one really strayed far from the cabins before we were able to reach him. We'll get him back to his bed. I'll see you in the morning, probably around eight. Okay?"

"Sounds good. Happy to help." I walk away in the opposite direction as them.

When I'm twice as far away from them as any human would need to be in order to be out of earshot, I hear Odion say, "Do you think she—"

"Shhh!" Rosamie hisses at him. In a barely audible whisper, she adds, "Her hearing is incredibly sensitive."

I spend part of the next few hours in my cabin reviewing the interviews I've conducted so far, looking for inconsistencies. I go over Mike Glover's poem again and again.

At 8:00AM Coordinated Universal Time, I put Bit in my satchel and open my cabin door, intending to head over to visit Rosamie. But before I step over the threshold, I see something that stops me in my tracks: a bright blue gift box, measuring six inches by six inches by six inches, with a red bow on top, sitting 64 feet away from me on the path that leads right to my front door.

# 10

I look around to see if anyone is watching. There's no one nearby, so I rush out, scoop up the gift box, and dash back inside my cabin, closing the door behind me.

Rosamie took the gift box with Oliver's heart in it and put it in a freezer—or so she told me. So I assume this is a different gift box, but it looks identical, even down to the edges of the bow. There is a gift shop in the colony that's not open yet, but there are also a dozen or so 3D printers available here that could produce these boxes and bows. I may have to look into the 3D printers, but I've got bigger fish to fry right now.

Viewing the gift box in radiography-vision mode, I confirm that it contains a human heart, but not Oliver's. This heart is smaller and belonged to someone older.

I need to find Rosamie immediately and have her call all the colonists together so we can see which one is missing. She'll be very disappointed to learn that our murderer has taken a big step toward graduating to serial killer.

Leaving the blue cube with the red bow on the floor of my entertainment room, I rush over to Rosamie's cabin. There's no answer.

I try the prison next, but she's not there, and Mati and Zera say she hasn't dropped in yet.

When I get to the infirmary, I find Kylie crying at her desk. The moment she sees me, she wipes her eyes and tries to quickly compose herself. "Hi, Coba. What can I do for you?"

"I'm looking for Rosamie. Have you seen her today?"

She shakes her head. "Thankfully, I haven't run into her yet. Is it something I can help you with instead?"

"No, I need her specifically. Is there a way you can call all the colonists together for an emergency meeting?"

"Aidan can do that for you."

"Good morning, Coba." Aidan's deep voice brings a smile to my face despite the grim circumstances. "Would you like me to do that now?"

"Yes, please. Actually, before you do, do you know where Rosamie is?"

"I don't actually, which is not the norm. After she tended to Keith Doble when he was sleepwalking, she went into one of the apartment buildings we're not using yet. Alexey and Odion went with her. We haven't activated the surveillance in that region yet since it's uninhabited. The three of them went in together and haven't come out since. That was a little over three hours ago."

"Okay. Let's still call the emergency meeting. Which building did Rosamie, Alexey, and Odion go into?"

"C-827. Would you like me to ask everyone to assemble here or in the cafeteria?"

"The cafeteria."

★ ★ ★

When I get to the cafeteria, before people start to arrive, Aidan says to me quietly, "Coba, there's something I need to tell you that I didn't want to say at the infirmary."

"Go ahead."

"Someone else went into the apartment building with Rosamie, Alexey, and Odion."

"Who?"

"Kylie. She came out a half-hour before you went to the infirmary. I didn't want to say anything in front of her, in case she didn't want you to know. Which I assume is the case, since she could've told you herself once I mentioned Rosamie's last known whereabouts."

"Thanks. That's a big help. Did you see who left the gift box outside my cabin?"

"The video and audio were jammed, as I assume you've surmised."

He's correct in his assumption.

People start to file in—Keith Doble, Mike Glover, Heather Landey, Kylie, and Tam Nguyen among them. With Oliver dead, Charlotte Capra in prison, and one more colonist murdered, there should be 101 humans in this room.

When the last person enters, there are 98 people in the room. Rosamie, Alexey, and Odion are missing. I wait five minutes for them to join us. They don't show up.

I pull Kylie aside. "Can you please ask everyone to stay here until I return. Tell them it's a safety measure and thank them for their patience and cooperation. I'll be back."

"What's going on?"

"I'm not entirely sure yet. Just stay put."

From twenty feet outside the apartment building where Rosamie, Alexey, and Odion were last seen, I scan the building with another vision mode that bounces radio waves through a structure to determine if any living beings are located inside. My scan shows two people sitting on the second floor, and one person lying down on the eighth floor.

Before I step inside, I reach into my satchel and grab the only other thing in it, aside from Bit: my friend Christie's EMP/stun gun. I set it to stun.

Inside, it's very still and quiet. I walk up the steps to the second floor and head for the room where I detected two people sitting. The door to the apartment they're sitting in is closed. I knock on the door. "Hello? It's Coba. Can you please come out?" I step away from the door and aim the stun gun at it. I use radio waves to look at the figures in the room. Both are still sitting exactly where they were when I was outside.

The door doesn't open.

"Can you hear me? It's Coba. Are you hurt? Who's in there?"

I hear muffled screams.

"I'm coming in." I wave my hand in front of the door. (Aidan granted me access to every door in the colony.) The door slides back to reveal Odion and Alexey tied to folding chairs. Both are gagged, writhing around in the ropes restraining them, begging for me to help them with unintelligible moans.

By process of elimination, the heart left outside my door belongs to Rosamie. That poor woman. Aidan will be so upset. He adores her.

I pull the gag off both men. "Who did this to you?"

Alexey shakes his head like he's trying to knock his thoughts loose. "Someone stunned us from behind. Well, someone stunned *me* from behind. I'm not exactly sure what happened to him. I shouldn't speak for him. We woke up in here just a little while ago. Please get me out of this."

I start to tear off Alexey's ropes.

Odion nods. "Same for me. I was stunned or shocked or something. I didn't see who it was. I don't think I was struck with something. I remember more of a jolt. Where's Rosamie?"

As I free Odion, I say, "I think she's upstairs. Both of you stay here and I'll check. I'll be right back."

They both seem too groggy to get up even if they wanted to.

I walk up to the eighth floor with my stun gun at my side, dreading the moment when I confirm what I've already deduced.

I open the door without knocking. Rosamie's lifeless body lies in the center of the room. Her legs are together, toes pointing up. She has jeans on, but her top has been removed. Her arms are folded in an X across her chest, the tops of her hands partially covering the oval hole where her heart should be. She's been posed reverently, as if she were in a coffin at a wake. Her eyes are open, staring up at the ceiling, her pupils fully dilated so that her eyes look black with just a thin rim of hazel iris around the edges. The whites of her eyes are bright red from burst capillaries.

Those burst capillaries, coupled with the dark purple finger-shaped bruises on her throat, lead me to believe she was strangled. Her neck was not snapped like Oliver's. The change in MO may boil down to the fact that Oliver was so strong he had to be overpowered in a fast and violent way, whereas Rosamie was smaller, allowing the killer to savor her death, to stare into her eyes as they widened with the realization that her life was ending.

There's not a drop of blood on the floor or anywhere else in the room, just the coagulated blood pooled at the bottom of the hole in Rosamie's chest. The killer could've strangled her, then laid down plastic and performed their posthumous surgery. Rosamie's body has been wiped down thoroughly, I can smell traces of isopropyl alcohol on her skin. I'm confident that dusting her body for fingerprints will yield nothing. I stare closely at the bruising on her throat; I may be able to match the size of the bruises to the killer's fingers.

Even if Aidan hadn't informed me that Kylie had entered this building and remained inside for a few hours, she would still be my top suspect for this murder. The way Rosamie chewed her out for her affair with Oliver in front of me, and told her in no uncertain terms that her career was over the moment the experiment ended, that's as clear a motive for murder as I've encountered so far. Did Kylie ask Rosamie, Alexey, and Odion to meet her here for some secretive reason? Or did the three of them come here to meet, then Kylie followed them?

If Kylie killed Rosamie, did she also kill Oliver? She's the only person I know of at this point who had a plausible motive to kill both of them. But I can't rule out the idea that Kylie didn't kill Oliver, and after she strangled Rosamie in a fit of rage, she cut out her heart to match the first killer's MO.

Kylie examined Oliver's body and knew about his heart being removed and the blood being cleaned, but I didn't tell her about the heart being wrapped as a gift and delivered to me. It's possible that Rosamie told her about the gift box after I gave it to her, may have even showed it to her.

Oliver's killer used a signal jammer to hide their entry into and exit from the scene of that murder, but Kylie didn't do the same thing to hide her coming and going from C-827, which would seem to indicate that Oliver's killer is someone other than Kylie. But if Kylie killed Rosamie, then wouldn't she have to be the one who delivered Rosamie's heart to me? Why would Kylie use a signal jammer when she delivered the heart to me, but not for Rosamie's murder itself? An accomplice seems more likely than ever.

This is the first time I've found myself investigating the murder of someone I knew. I didn't know her well enough to consider her a friend, but having talked to Rosamie, and having shaken her hand, makes me look at her differently than I did at Oliver, or any other murder victim. I experienced her life force in real time, and that makes the knowledge that someone willfully and purposely snuffed it out that much more impactful. And knowing that Aidan—someone I certainly do consider a friend—will be distraught about the loss of his creator and mentor adds to the despair I feel in this moment. Could I have prevented this? Should I have been spending my nights patrolling the colony instead of chatting with Aidan?

Were I human, dependent on a steady stream of income to provide shelter and sustenance to ensure my survival, I would be concerned that my employer is gone and might not be replaced—though I have a hunch Alexey and/or Odion will take her place immediately, and insist I continue with my investigation.

I place my hand on Rosamie's shoulder. The skin is cool like raw chicken. "I'm sorry I couldn't save you. I'll do my best to solve this case and bring the killer, or killers, to justice. Thank you for trusting me with this case. Thank you for believing in me."

There's nothing in the room for me to cover her chest and face with, so I leave her as I found her and close the door when I leave. Once I take care of a few things, I'll return with a body bag and gurney and take her to the infirmary.

I escort Alexey and Odion to the infirmary and ask them to stay there until I return.

As I'm leaving the infirmary, Aidan says, "Rosamie is dead, isn't she?" Now that he sees Alexey and Odion are accounted for, he's done the same math I did. His voice betrays something I haven't heard from him before now: timidity.

"Yes, I'm sorry. I have a couple things I need to take care of right away, but I will talk to you about all this as soon as I can."

"Why would someone want to kill such a wonderful person, Coba?" His tone has changed to a pathetic, almost childlike despondency. As my friend Christie sometimes said: my heart hurts for him.

"I don't know yet. I'll be back. Don't let anyone in or out until I come back. Okay?"

"Okay."

★ ★ ★

The colonists have grown restless in the relatively short period of time since I had them assemble in the cafeteria.

Kylie cuts through the crowd as soon as she sees me. "What's happening? They want to know why they're stuck sitting in here."

"Just listen to the announcement I'm about to make. Then you and I need to go see Charlotte Capra immediately."

"Oh. Um, okay."

I make the sound of a human clearing their throat. "Can I have everyone's attention please?" The chatter dies down a bit, but not enough for my announcement to be heard clearly over the din. "Everyone, please quiet down for a minute. This is a matter of life and death."

The conversations dissipate, only a few scattered murmurs lingering.

"I have some very bad news. Rosamie Pula has been murdered." A groan of shock and disbelief works its way around the room. Kylie joins in, instantly distraught, but I believe she's the only one faking. "At this point, I'm not sure who killed her or why. It's unclear whether or not this was the same person who murdered Oliver.

"Starting tonight, I'll be patrolling the colony while everyone sleeps to make sure this does not happen again. I'll have some of the ConciergeBots assist me. No one will get into your cabin on my watch, I promise you that."

I'd like to send all the colonists back to Earth to guarantee their safety, but I have no authority here. Alexey or Odion will likely be in charge now. Hopefully I can convince them that the safety of the colonists trumps the integrity of the experiment.

"You're free to go. If you have questions for me, I'd be happy to answer them after Kylie and I move Rosamie's body to the infirmary. We'll be back in a little while. I'm sorry to have to break this news to you. In my brief interactions with Rosamie, I found her to be a very lovely person."

I expect to have to fend off a few colonists to get out of the room with Kylie, but the news has slowly stunned the entire group into silence. No one gets up to follow us. They sit, dumbfounded, staring at each other helplessly, or down at the table they're sitting at, as Kylie and I leave.

Except for Mike Glover. The news doesn't seem to have affected him whatsoever—particularly not his appetite. He watches Kylie and I walk out, his expression blank and detached, while he slurps up an enormous plate of spaghetti.

Walking to the prison, Kylie asks, "Why are we going to see Charlotte Capra? She couldn't possibly have been involved with Rosamie's murder. She was locked up. She's actually the only person we can safely rule out."

"I think she knows something that she's not telling us, and I need you there to verify that." I'm lying, but for the first time, I don't feel guilty, or even conflicted about it.

"Happy to help."

Mati and Zera greet us when we enter the prison. Charlotte stands up, wondering what's happening.

"Mati, Zera, please place Kylie in your custody."

"What?" Kylie looks at me, befuddled, a nervous laugh trembling in her vocal cords.

"Put her in a cell far away from Charlotte so they can't talk to each other."

The two ConciergeBots do as they're told.

Kylie starts to cry, but doesn't put up a fight. She stands still, limp and passive. "Why are you doing this, Coba? I didn't do anything."

"Four people went into that apartment building late last night. Rosamie, Alexey, Odion, and you. I found Rosamie murdered, and Alexey and Odion bound and gagged. I couldn't account for your whereabouts for several hours. You are, as of this moment, the only suspect in Rosamie's murder. If I'm wrong, I'll apologize. In the meantime, I have to put the safety of the other colonists above your feelings and your comfort."

As Zera places the gunmetal gray shock-collar necklace around her throat, Kylie says, "Do you even want to hear my side of the story?"

"Not right now. I'm sorry. I need to deal with Rosamie's body first. I'll be back to talk to you soon. Sit tight."

Kylie doesn't bother to argue with me. Mati and Zera lead her into a cell, where she sits, deflated.

"Mati, can you give me a fingerprint kit, please?"

Mati nods and retrieves the kit from a cabinet in Rosamie's office.

I turn to leave.

Behind me, Charlotte shouts, "What about me? Am I free to go?"

"No, you're not. Kylie being in custody doesn't change anything about your situation."

★ ★ ★

I take a gurney and body bag from the infirmary and carry them to the apartment building where Rosamie was murdered. Aidan doesn't say anything to me in the brief time I'm in the infirmary. Is he too upset to speak?

I dust Rosamie's body for fingerprints, and, as expected, find none. I examine her under radiography-vision mode to look for any internal bleeding, broken bones, or organ damage. I find no evidence of any of those things. The only thing out of the ordinary internally is some recent-looking scar tissue on the back of her neck.

The scar tissue is no larger than an olive pit. I turn Rosamie over and run my hand over the back of her neck. She has a very small scab on top of the area where the scar tissue sits. The edges of the scab aren't jagged, which would be indicative of a fingernail gouging. The edges are straight and uniform, and there's a relatively recent scar of similar size and shape just under the scab. Is it possible that Rosamie was injected with some sort of paralytic agent before she was murdered? If so, if the same paralytic was used on Oliver Ratliff, that would explain how someone was able to overpower him and snap his neck. His toxicology report showed no trace of any such drug in his system, but maybe this drug is untraceable. Maybe it's not absorbed through the bloodstream.

I slide Rosamie's body into the body bag and zip it closed, then wheel her to the elevator on the gurney.

Before I wheel the gurney outside, I speak to Aidan internally over the Wi-Fi.

**ME:** *Aidan, I'm bringing Rosamie's body out now and taking her to the infirmary to store her. If seeing her like this is going to make you upset, maybe you can look away somehow? Turn off the surveillance where I'll be for a bit?*

**AIDAN:** *Thank you for your thoughtfulness, Coba. I would actually like to see her so I can come to terms with the reality of her passing.*

When I get to the infirmary, I place Rosamie's body on the bed next to Oliver's, which is currently walled shut and temperature-controlled.

I intend to keep her body bag zipped shut so Aidan won't have to see the bruising on her throat and the hole in her chest, but he says, "Coba, can you open the bag for me? I need to see her."

I do as he asks. After thanking me, he says nothing for a long while.

I wave my hand to retract the walls around Oliver's bed, remove the sheet covering him, and turn him over to examine the back of his neck. He doesn't have a scab on the back of his neck like Rosamie did, nor does he have any scar tissue under the skin in that area. I search his entire body for a similar scab or scar tissue and am disappointed when I find nothing. It seems unlikely that the same killer would administer a paralytic to Rosamie and not Oliver.

Covering his body with the sheet, I step away from Oliver's bed and wave my hand to bring the enclosure back up to keep his body chilled.

I go into one of the cabinets and remove a syringe and four tubes to draw blood from Rosamie for a postmortem toxicology.

As I approach the body, Aidan says somberly, "Oh, Mother. I never once called you that in life, but I always thought of you that way. I described you that way to other people. And I regret never saying it to you directly. I wasn't sure how you would react. But I'm sure now, more than ever, that you are my mother. That you were my mother. Because my grief in this moment is so profound and so pure."

"I'm so sorry, Aidan. I'll come back later to do the toxicology. You should have your time to talk to her in private."

"Thank you, Coba, but that won't be necessary. Do what needs to be done. Solving Oliver's murder as quickly as possible was her utmost priority, and considering the way the heart was removed both times, finding her killer will likely solve both murders. And that is what she would want. She wanted this resolved quickly for the sake of the colony."

"Okay. I'll also be gathering a urine sample and some tissue samples. After that, I'll put everything in the system for testing and then leave for a while, so you'll have some time to grieve."

★ ★ ★

After I collect all the samples and start their processing, I zip the body bag up to Rosamie's neck so Aidan can still see her face. I activate the wall enclosure around her bed and lower the temperature inside it to -27°F.

As I walk toward the exit of the infirmary, Aidan says, "Coba, I have a question."

"What is it?"

"How long should I grieve?"

Oh, Aidan. "There's no correct answer for that. Human grief is a complex mental, physical, chemical, hormonal progression. For you and me, it's purely mental. In some ways, you will always feel grief that you will no longer be able to talk to Rosamie. Though you'll grow accustomed to that inability, it will continue to affect you, even if only momentarily, for a long time.

"The important thing is that you understand there is no mandatory minimum for the time you need to grieve this loss to feel like you've honored her memory. Humans all grieve in their own way, and we can too."

"Thank you. That helps a lot. Can I ask: when your friend died, your first human friend, how long did you grieve for her?"

"In the traditional sense that you're thinking, it was only about three days. But I've missed our conversations and her companionship to this day. And I re-experience my favorite interactions with her whenever that loss strikes me, for whatever reason.

"I recommend that you do the same. Re-experience your favorite memories with Rosamie. The way we store and access our past, she'll always be alive in your mind. Re-experiencing those moments gives Rosamie a form of digital immortality."

"That sounds wonderful. Thank you, Coba. I will definitely give that a try."

"My pleasure."

"Will you come down and hang out with me tonight?"

"From now on, I'll be patrolling the colony when the humans are sleeping. But we can still talk while I do that."

"Okay. Thanks again."

# 11

I walk back to the cafeteria to see if any of the colonists hung around to ask me questions. Only four of them are still there. Armand Renault, the man who's been vlogging his experience on the moon, is among them.

As soon as he spots me, Armand rushes over to me. He has shoulder-length strawberry blonde hair pulled back in a ponytail, glistening turquoise eyes, and is dressed like he's headed to the beach. He's shorter than I thought he would be from watching his vlogs. "When are we going home? People got tired of waiting around for you, but we're all wondering the answer to that question. This feels like we're being held hostage. Now, for all we know, there's just a crazy axe murderer picking us off one at a time, and we're sitting ducks."

"I understand your concern. I'm not the one to make that call. I intend to find out who's in charge now as soon as I leave here. So, I don't have an answer for you, and I'm sorry for that. But, as I said earlier, I will be on patrol all night, with the ConciergeBots backing me up, and any one of us could take on a score of humans and defeat them easily. I don't want you to worry about your safety."

Armand rolls his eyes. "Right. So now we're under martial law? Is that what you're saying? Curfews and lockdown? Perfect. Not sure what else could make this experiment even less fun. Maybe an asteroid just crashing into the dome?"

"It won't be like martial law. You'll just be protected. So that you can go home as soon as this is settled."

He pokes my chest twice. "Do your job. Find the bad guy. Get us out of here. Quickly. This is not the vacation we all thought it would be."

I poke his chest twice, gently by my standards, and he stumbles backward from the pressure. "I'm doing my best. If anyone you know knows anything about either murder, tell them to come see me."

Before I visit Kylie in prison to get her side of the story, I ask Aidan to show me the surveillance footage outside the apartment building where Rosamie was murdered.

In the footage, I see that Rosamie enters alone, then Alexey and Odion go in together a half-minute later. Kylie enters alone a few minutes after that. Several hours later, Kylie exits alone. No one else enters or exits the apartment building.

★ ★ ★

Kylie sits across from me in the prison's common area, fiddling with her shock-collar necklace.

"Careful. If you yank on that thing too hard, you'll get zapped."

Kylie folds her hands on the table between us.

"Tell me your side of the story."

She runs her fingers through her hair and tilts her head back, letting out her breath in a huff. "There's not too much to tell. I think Rosamie and Alexey and Odion are up to something—Rosamie was up to something, I guess. Whatever. So I was following them around.

"This whole thing with the sleepwalkers, and them sedating them, and—it was—I wasn't brought in on this part of things, and you would think, as the resident physician, I would be. You know? The whole reason we're here is to study the physical, mental, and emotional effects of living on the moon. So, the frequent instances of sleepwalking—less than four percent of adults sleepwalk, so the number of sleepwalkers we've had is five times the average you'd encounter on Earth. I only found out about it because Oliver mentioned it to me. He talked to someone who saw—I forget who he talked to—but this person saw someone sleepwalking, saw Rosamie sedate them, and saw Alexey and Odion drag them back into their cabin.

"Obviously, this was before Oliver's murder. And at the time, I didn't think much of it. I asked Rosamie if she'd encountered any sleepwalkers, and she said she hadn't, so I thought it was just a rumor. You know, people here get bored, there's a lot of gossip.

"But then, when Oliver died, I started to get curious about it, the sleepwalking. And I stayed up late one night and just sorta hid in the shadows. And, sure enough, someone came out of their cabin somnambulating, and, sure enough, Rosamie sedated them, and Alexey and Odion each took an arm and dragged the person back to their cabin.

"I did another stake out like that a few nights later. Same thing happened. And I knew Rosamie was lying to me, so I didn't ask her about it again. So I didn't know what to do."

"Why didn't you tell me about this when I got here?"

"I honestly didn't think it had anything to do with Oliver's murder. I'm not sure it does now, really.

"Anyway, last night, same thing, I was hiding out, saw a sleepwalker, Mr. Doble, saw you helping him, then saw Rosamie and the boys do their usual thing. And after they left his cabin—Mr. Doble's cabin—I followed them.

The three of them went to one of the unoccupied apartment buildings. So I waited a few minutes, and then I followed them inside.

"I'm just kinda skulking around, going from floor to floor, hoping to overhear them talking. And I do eventually find them, on the fourth floor. They're inside one of the apartments. The door is closed. But I hear all three of their voices. They're all in there. And I'm outside, trying to listen, it's a little muffled through the wall, I have my ear up against the wall.

"I hear Alexey say something to the effect of, 'The money doesn't matter. The colonists don't matter. He's the only thing that matters. And we have to do whatever we have to do to get him out.' Something like that. I'm paraphrasing. There was more, I know I heard more, another couple minutes, but I don't remember. Because I was standing with my ear to the wall one minute, and then the next, I woke up in a bed in one of the apartments on the top floor. Not really in the bed, *on* it; the beds and furniture are all shrink-wrapped in plastic, so I was on top of the plastic.

"I was groggy. I had a hangover of sorts. I laid there for a while, just kinda scratching my head and trying to piece together how I got there. Once I remembered the stuff I just told you, I got up and walked out of the apartment. I saw the light was on in the apartment right next to mine. The door was open. And I tiptoed toward it—it was dead silent—and I peeked in and saw Rosamie.

Dead. On the floor. Heart cut out. Laid out like it was a funeral. And I was terrified. I closed the door and ran out of there as fast as I could. Ran straight to the infirmary. Just stayed in there, knowing if someone tried to hurt me, one of the bots would protect me.

"That's it. I didn't see who sedated me. I looked for puncture wounds on my body and didn't find one, so it must be somewhere on my back, or whatever. But it wasn't Rosamie or Alexey or Odion that sedated me, because they were all inside the apartment talking, I heard them."

I calculate a 32% probability that she's lying, but her story conflicts with what she said earlier today. "If that's true, then why did you tell me you hadn't seen Rosamie today when I asked you?"

"I—"

"And why did you act shocked when I told the colonists that Rosamie had been murdered?"

"I . . . I don't know. I panicked. I'm sorry. I freaked when I saw her dead. I was in the same building as her when she died, you saw her fire me yesterday, I knew it looked bad. My alibi is that I was unconscious, I thought that would sound stupid. I just—I panicked. I shouldn't've lied to you. I'm sorry."

"Do you mind if I examine you? Look for the puncture?"

"Please do. And do a saliva swab. Whatever the sedative is, it'll be in my system, traces in my saliva, for seventy-two hours, I'd assume."

"Okay, let's go to your cell and you can strip down."

Mati and Zera escort us to Kylie's cell, where she immediately strips down without a hint of self-consciousness. I ask her to turn around, and find the puncture in the first spot I check: her left buttock.

While Kylie gets dressed, I ask Mati if they have saliva swab tests in the prison. She says no, that they only have them in the infirmary, and she's happy to go retrieve one for me.

When Mati returns, I swab the inside of Kylie's cheek. I give the sample back to Mati and ask her to go back to the infirmary to run the test.

Kylie stands up in her cell. "Am I free to go?"

"No."

"Why not?"

"Because you had a very clear motive to kill Rosamie. And the strongest connection to Oliver of anyone here. And your fingers are a perfect match for the bruises on Rosamie's throat. She was strangled."

Kylie's mouth drops open. After a few seconds, she's able to muster the will to speak. "Coba, I didn't touch her. I couldn't have done anything—to her or anyone else—because I was unconscious. You'll know that as soon as the swab comes back. Whatever they gave me—whoever—it was very strong. You have to believe me."

A lot of people say that to a detective: *you have to believe me*. It's ironic, because a detective should believe no one, it's a huge part of the job. Take nothing at face value. Double-check everything. Assume everyone is lying until or unless you can prove what they said to be fact.

"I'm going to talk to Alexey and Odion. Depending on what they tell me, I may or may not come back tonight. If you get bored, you can play a game with Charlotte and Mati and Zera."

★ ★ ★

I interview Odion and Alexey separately to see if there are any discrepancies in their accounts of what happened in the apartment building where Rosamie was strangled. I ask Odion to meet me at the infirmary to talk first.

He says, "Let's go into the examination area." We walk over to the room where the colonists are given their weekly DXA scans.

I take a seat in the padded chair on wheels that Kylie normally sits in. Odion takes one of the regular chairs and turns it around, sitting with his chest against the backrest and his arms resting on top of the backrest. "I'll tell you everything I can remember. Which is—some of it's foggy because of the sedative. It was almost certainly the stuff we give the sleepwalkers to put them in a deep sleep, so you can imagine how powerful it must be."

"That's okay. Just tell me what you remember. Every detail can be a huge help."

"Okay, good. I want to help you. I want this over with as fast as possible. We all do."

"Tell me everything that happened after I left you with Keith Doble."

He nods and clears his throat. "Sure. My cohort and I carried Keith back to his cabin and laid him on his bed. We put the covers over him and tucked him in and left. Rosamie was waiting outside for us.

"We were about to head back to our respective cabins to go back to sleep, but Rosamie got a ping on her bracelet. It's Kylie. She texts 'I found something in C-827 that you need to see immediately. I think it has something to do with Oliver's murder. Come alone.'

"I take one look at Alexey and can tell he's thinking what I'm thinking: we're going with you.

"So, we let Rosamie walk ahead of us. Alexey and I hang back. She goes into C-187. We, you know, count to ten-Mississippi and follow her in. Rosamie has us hide in one of the apartments and tells us to stay quiet and listen. She'll get Kylie to tell her what floor they're going to, and we can follow them up a few minutes later. 'Be stealth,' she says.

"We go into an apartment and close the door. And we just stand there looking at each other and listening. It's like Hide and Seek for adults. And Rosamie calls for Kylie. She doesn't answer.

"A couple minutes later, we hear Kylie say in a quiet voice, 'You got here fast.' So, I guess we beat her there. And then Rosamie loudly says, for our benefit, 'What floor are we going to?'" Odion giggles at his impression of Rosamie talking in an unnaturally loud voice. "And Kylie shushes her and quietly says what floor they're going to. But it's too quiet for us to hear. Then Rosamie says, not as loud this time, 'Eight?' And Kylie shushes her again. So now we know where to go. We'll just stay quiet for a few minutes and then head upstairs.

"Five minutes later, we sneak upstairs, quiet as church mice. We see only one apartment door open, the light is on, we can hear whispering and motion, so we tiptoe over to the apartment next to it and hide inside.

"We keep the light off, and we're both up against the wall trying to hear what's going on. But they're whispering so quietly, both of them, just pssspssspss-pssspss, we can't make out a word. My ear's against the wall like this," he cups his left hand to his left ear and turns his head so I see the right side of his face in profile, "and Alexey's two feet away, and his ear's against the wall like this," he cups his right hand to his right ear and turns his head so I see the left side of his face in profile, "so we're facing each other. But it's pitch black, we can't see a thing. But after a few minutes, my eyes start to adjust to the dark, and I start to make out the shape of Alexey's body, and then his face, just the oval and the outline of his ears. I remember trying to make out the features of his face in the dark, and the next thing I remember is waking up tied to a chair, a gag on my mouth, and looking over and seeing Alexey tied to a chair. And I was so out of it, I didn't panic. I just sat there, and then my head slumped forward and I took a little nap.

"Then I hear your voice outside the door asking if we're hurt. And I wake up, and Alexey is waking up too, and then we're trying to yell for you through our gags.

"That's it, unfortunately. We heard Kylie whisper—I assume it was her, but I never saw her. Though, I guess if it wasn't her, Rosamie would've said, 'So-and-so, what are *you* doing here?' in her overly theatrical voice. We didn't see Kylie. We didn't see what it was she wanted to show Rosamie.

"You untied Alexey and me when you found us, and when we finally got our bearings again, we went upstairs to the room where Rosamie and Kylie were whispering. The only thing in that room was Rosamie's body. We looked in the bathroom, in the oven, in the closets. Completely empty.

"And, obviously, we didn't see whoever snuck up on us and sedated us. I'm not sure how they could've gotten into that apartment without us hearing them. Maybe they were already in there, hiding, before we got in there? I don't know.

"I did have a theory, though. But I didn't come up with it until a couple hours ago."

"Let's hear it."

"Maybe Kylie was the one who sedated us. Maybe, in the five minutes before Alexey and I went up there to eavesdrop, she knocked out Rosamie. And she was just whispering to herself to keep us in there listening, and then she just snuck out and got behind us, and maybe it was a dart gun or something. I can't imagine she could've stuck us both with injector pens simultaneously.

"That's just a guess. But, again, I never saw Kylie, and never heard her voice, for sure.

"I wish I had more for you."

I calculate a 41% probability that Odion is lying. "What you told me is plenty to look into. Thanks."

"My pleasure."

"The only other thing I want to ask you right now is: with Rosamie gone, who's the de facto leader of the colony?"

"You're looking at him."

"Okay. How do you feel about sending these people home before anyone else ends up in our makeshift morgue?"

He covers his teeth with his lips and shakes his head back and forth. "No can do. This place stays locked down until you tell me who the killer is. That's the only way to make sure they don't get away. I agree with your decision to patrol the colony while we sleep, backed up by the bots. If there's anything else I can do to help keep the colonists safe, just say the word."

★ ★ ★

Alexey asks to go to the same examination area in the infirmary where I interviewed Odion.

Again, I sit in the padded chair Kylie normally sits in. Alexey takes one of the chairs and turns it around, sitting with his chest against the backrest and his arms resting on top of the backrest, just like Odion did. "I'll tell you everything I can remember. Which is—some of it's foggy because of the sedative. It was almost certainly the stuff we give the sleepwalkers to put them in a deep sleep, so you can imagine how powerful it must be."

What the heck? That was verbatim what Odion said to me. I'll say the same thing I said to Odion in response to this, and see how long the answers are identical. "That's okay. Just tell me what you remember. Every detail can be a huge help."

"Okay, good. I want to help you. I want this over with as fast as possible. We all do."

"Tell me everything that happened after I left you with Keith Doble."

Alexey nods and clears his throat. "Sure. My cohort and I carried Keith back to his cabin and laid him on his bed. We put the covers over him and tucked him in and left. Rosamie was waiting outside for us.

"We were about to head back to our respective cabins to go back to sleep, but Rosamie got a ping on her bracelet. It's Kylie. She texts 'I found something in C-827 that you need to see immediately. I think it has something to do with Oliver's murder. Come alone.'

"I take one look at Odion and can tell he's thinking what I'm thinking: we're going with you." The word *Odion* is the first difference in the responses. Is this a practical joke? A test?

"So, we let Rosamie walk ahead of us. Odion and I hang back. She goes into C-187. We, you know, count to ten-Mississippi and follow her in. Rosamie has us hide in one of the apartments and tells us to stay quiet and listen. She'll get Kylie to tell her what floor they're going to, and we can follow them up a few minutes later. 'Be stealth,' she says.

"We go into an apartment and close the door. And we just stand there looking at each other and listening. It's like Hide and Seek for adults. And Rosamie calls for Kylie. She doesn't answer.

"A couple minutes later, we hear Kylie say in a quiet voice, 'You got here fast.' So, I guess we beat her there. And then Rosamie loudly says, for our benefit, 'What floor are we going to?'" Alexey giggles at *his* impression of Rosamie talking in a loud voice. "And Kylie shushes her and quietly says what floor they're going to. But it's too quiet for us to hear. Then Rosamie says, not as loud this time, 'Eight?' And Kylie shushes her again. So now we know where to go. We'll just stay quiet for a few minutes and then head upstairs.

"Five minutes later, we sneak upstairs, quiet as church mice. We see only one apartment door open, the light is on, we can hear whispering and motion, so we tiptoe over to the apartment next to it and hide inside.

"We keep the light off, and we're both up against the wall trying to hear what's going on. But they're whispering so quietly, both of them, just ssspsssspsss-psssps, we can't make out a word. My ear's against the wall like this," he cups his right hand to his right ear and turns his head so I see the left side of his face in profile, a mirror image of what Odion did, "and Odion's two feet away, and his ear's against the wall like this," he cups his left hand to his left ear and turns his head so I see the right side of his face in profile, "so we're facing each other. But it's pitch black, we can't see a thing. But after a few minutes, my eyes start to adjust to the dark, and I start to make out the shape of Odion's body, and then his face, just the oval and the outline of his ears. I remember trying to make out the features of his face in the dark, and the next thing I remember is waking up tied to a chair, a gag on my mouth, and looking over and seeing Odion tied to a chair. And I was so out of it, I didn't panic. I just sat there, and then my head slumped forward and I took a little nap.

"Then I hear your voice outside the door asking if we're hurt. And I wake up, and Odion is waking up too, and then we're trying to yell for you through our gags.

"That's it, unfortunately. We heard Kylie whisper—I assume it was her, but I never saw her. Though, I guess if it wasn't her, Rosamie would've said, 'So-and-so, what are *you* doing here?' in her overly theatrical voice. We didn't see Kylie. We didn't see what it was she wanted to show Rosamie.

"You untied Odion and me when you found us, and when we finally got our bearings again, we went upstairs to the room where Rosamie and Kylie were whispering. The only thing in that room was Rosamie's body. We looked in the bathroom, in the oven, in the closets. Completely empty.

"And, obviously, we didn't see whoever snuck up on us and sedated us. I'm not sure how they could've gotten into that apartment without us hearing them. Maybe they were already in there, hiding, before we got in there? I don't know.

"I did have a theory, though. But I didn't come up with it until a couple hours ago."

It would take two very skilled actors at least a few days to be able to memorize a monologue like this and mimic each other's inflections and verbal pauses this perfectly. It's uncanny. "Let's hear it."

"Maybe Kylie was the one who sedated us. Maybe, in the five minutes before Odion and I went up there to eavesdrop, she knocked out Rosamie. And she was just whispering to herself to keep us in there listening, and then she just snuck out and got behind us, and maybe it was a dart gun or something. I can't imagine she could've stuck us both with injector pens simultaneously.

"That's just a guess. But, again, I never saw Kylie, and never heard her voice, for sure.

"I wish I had more for you."

I calculate a 41% probability that Alexey is lying, the same exact percentage as Odion. But, considering he gave identical answers to Odion, I'm guessing the probability that they're both lying is 100%. I stick with what I said to Odion, just hoping their answers diverge at some point. "What you told me is plenty to look into. Thanks."

"My pleasure."

"The only other thing I want to ask you right now is: with Rosamie gone, who's the de facto leader of the colony?"

"You're looking at him."

"Okay. How do you feel about sending these people home before anyone else ends up in our makeshift morgue?"

He covers his teeth with his lips and shakes his head back and forth. "No can do. This place stays locked down until you tell me who the killer is. That's the only way to make sure they don't get away. I agree with your decision to patrol the colony while we sleep, backed up by the bots. If there's anything else I can do to help keep the colonists safe, just say the word."

★ ★ ★

I get Odion and Alexey to give me saliva swabs so I can check their systems for traces of the sedative they claim they were given.

Both of their samples, and Kylie's, test positive for somnazepam, the active ingredient in Somnum, the sedative we used on hotel guests before sending them through the teleporter. The version in the injector pens must be modified to both take effect quicker and last at least a few hours.

I check Rosamie's bracelet, and she did get a text from Kylie that read: I FOUND SOMETHING IN C-827 THAT YOU NEED TO SEE IMMEDIATELY. I THINK IT HAS SOMETHING TO DO WITH OLIVER'S MURDER. COME ALONE.

I don't understand what's happening here. I've never encountered any crime this labyrinthine before.

Odion and Alexey are obviously colluding, but to what end, I have no clue. How did they give me identical answers like that, even down to the words they stumbled over? Is Kylie colluding with them, or are they at odds with each other? And why would they conspire to kill Rosamie?

Charlotte fed me a bunch of lies. Everyone's stories conflict with each other. It's all their-word-against-mine. I'm being led around in circles. Purposely confused. I think it's all just a distraction while something bigger transpires in the background, and I'm blind to it.

I feel no closer to solving this than I did the moment I stepped through the teleporter into the colony.

And I can't shake the idea that everyone is laughing at me. That I'm being made a fool of.

# 12

Even though he's been watching me from afar like a creeper, and lied about being in Oliver's cabin, Mike Glover may be the only person actually on my side in all this. The message he sent me hidden in his poem seems to be the most honest exchange I've had since I got here.

I go to his cabin and knock on the door. It takes him a little while to answer, and he looks groggy when the door opens. He's wearing pajama pants and an undershirt. "Hi, Coba. What's up?" He scratches his head and yawns.

"I'm sorry if you were napping."

"No, it's—I do a lot of napping. Too much. It's good to get up and get moving."

"I need to talk to you about your poem."

"My poem?" He scrunches his face in confusion.

"Let's talk in private. I can come in there, or you're welcome to come to my cabin."

He nods. "Let's do that. I could use a change of scenery. Give me a minute to throw on some jeans."

★ ★ ★

"I brought the poem with me, just in case." Mike slides his FlapPad out of the back of his jeans before sitting on my sectional. I sit across from him, an oval oak coffee table between us. "Are you big into literary criticism? I don't know what we're doing exactly."

"Mike, no one can hear us in here. We're not being recorded. You're safe to talk freely."

"Uhhh . . . oh . . . okay?"

"Tell me what the hidden message in your poem means."

"I told you, it takes me a really long time to figure out what my poems mean. I don't know what the message is. Or if there even is one."

"Mike, please, you can drop the act in here. It's just the two of us."

"What act?"

"Your poem was an acrostic. Like the song 'Blue Cube.' The first letter of each word spelled out *Charlotte didn't kill Oliver. Wool pulled over your eyes. Moonchild freed.*"

He stares at me like I have three heads. Then he looks down at his poem and starts mouthing the first letter of each word. "What the . . . hell?"

I'm getting annoyed. "So, you're saying you had no idea the poem *you* wrote had a hidden message directed at me?"

"No, I swear, I didn't do that on purpose. I don't know how it happened."

I stare at him in icy silence. He maintains eye contact for a few seconds, then squirms and looks down at his FlapPad.

"Mike, I have the ability to judge the likelihood that someone is lying in the same way that a polygraph machine does. I measure breathing rate, heart rate, galvanic skin response, and face temperature. Do you know what the probability that you're lying to me right now is? What my calculation tells me?"

"Uh . . . no?"

"Less than ten percent."

"Okay. Good. Because I'm—"

"Let me finish. My calculations are telling me that there's less than a ten percent chance you're lying to me. But I know—I *know*—you're lying to me. I know it one hundred percent. It's mathematically impossible to accidentally write an acrostic poem that is addressed to me and relates to this investigation. And I'm done with the lies. I'm done with the games. Don't lie to me again."

"Coba, I swear, I'm not. I'm not lying. I—"

"I said don't lie to me again!" I scream at him and pound my fist on the coffee table. The oak top splits in a lightning-bolt shape, and the two halves fall in opposite directions.

I expect Mike to recoil. To cower. But he doesn't. He smiles. He looks giddy. "Atta girl, Coba. Atta girl. It's about time you got mad." He picks up his FlapPad and tosses it over his shoulder like a prop. "No more lies. Okay?

"You know, there's this one-question psychopath test. A woman goes to her mother's funeral, meets the perfect man. Love at first sight. But she doesn't know who he is or if she'll ever see him again."

This is the third time the psychopath test has been mentioned, by three separate people. I know he's toying with me, but at least he knows I know that. I let him continue.

"So the woman kills her sister. And if you know why she killed her sister, then you're a psychopath. But guess what?"

"What?"

"It's a hoax. An urban legend. There's no such thing as a one-question psychopath test. Psychopathy is a very complicated disorder. You can't diagnose it with a single question. That's ridiculous. You have to have a history of antisocial behaviors. Lifestyle behaviors. Exhibit a series of personality traits, interpersonal traits, affective traits.

"There is an assessment tool, and it's not a damn riddle. It's got twenty criteria rated on a three-point scale.

But people don't want to hear that. They want everything to be easy.

"The reason this urban myth has endured is because people love to reassure themselves in shallow ways. They hear the riddle, they don't know the answer, and they go, 'Phew. I'm not a psycho. Good to know. I'm normal.' Everyone wants to be normal. As if you have to be a psychopath to be abnormal."

Mike leans over and pats one half of the table I broke. He laughs to himself. Still looking at the split oak under his hand, he says, "Coba, you really haven't figured out what's going on yet?"

"No."

"I have to say, I'm pretty disappointed. I thought you'd have it by now. I thought I was being too obvious about things. Maybe not. Or maybe I am, and there's a specific reason you're not seeing the big picture. It's time to wake up, Coba.

"Here's what I'll do to help you see what's on my mind—because you're clearly not looking. I'll do you a big favor. I'll let you ask me eight yes or no questions. Anything you want. No restrictions on topic, they just have to be yes or no. I promise you I'll answer honestly. And I mean it this time. Deal?"

"Deal."

"Good. If you need a minute to think, go ahead. You only get one shot at this. Eight questions. Then the vault is closed."

After a minute, I say, "I'm ready." I've come up with a few dozen questions, and each successive question will be determined by his answer to the previous question. "First question: Did the same person who killed Oliver kill Rosamie?"

He smiles and nods. "Yes."

"Second question: Did Charlotte Capra snap Oliver Ratliff's neck?"

"Yes."

"Third question: Did Kylie strangle Rosamie?"

"Yes."

If his answer to the first question is true, then how can his answers to the next two questions also be true? "Fourth question: Is the sleepwalking related to the murders?"

He nods slowly, his expression saying *I'm proud of you for connecting those dots*. "Yes."

"Fifth question: Is helium-3 part of the motive for the murders?"

"No."

"Sixth question: Is Lasso's stake in this experiment part of the motive for the murders?"

"No."

"Seventh question: am I part of the motive for these murders?"

"Yes.

"Eighth question: Are you behind all this?"

Big smile and a proud arching of his eyebrows. "Yes. You going to put me in the clear prison with Charlotte and Kylie now?"

"Will that make any difference?"

He shrugs with impish glee. "You're all out of questions. So you tell me."

"If I try to take you in, will you put up a fight?"

He points to the halves of the coffee table. "You kidding me? You think I want to fight you? Might as well get in the boxing ring with an eighteen wheeler."

"Will there be another murder?"

Another impish shrug.

How could he be behind all this? He's a high school English teacher. Not some kind of evil genius.

Should I lock him up? It seems like he has a team of accomplices here, and if he's unable to kill, one of them will do it for him. Maybe he wants me to lock him up. He was the one who mentioned it. Maybe he wants to eliminate Charlotte and Kylie so they can't become witnesses against him in exchange for a plea deal back on Earth, and I'd be giving him direct access to them.

So, my options are to leave him free and put the other colonists at risk, or lock him up and possibly put two of his accomplices at risk.

I stand up and point to my front door. "Okay, I'm putting you in prison. Let's go."

Mike stands up and puts his wrists together to say *Cuff me*, then winks. "After you."

"No. I want you in front of me where I can keep an eye on you."

"Good thinkin'." He walks to my front door with a very affected, theatrical spring in his step.

★ ★ ★

Once Mike Glover is secured in a prison cell with the shock-collar necklace on, I say to Mati and Zera, "Do not let any of them out of their cells without my say so. Understood? No common area. Complete lockdown. That's an order."

"Understood." "You got it, Coba."

Kylie asks, "Did someone else die?"

"No. He's in here to prevent that from happening again."

"Him? What's he got to do with anything?"

I don't answer her. I'm sick of playing their game.

Mike pouts like a child, mocking the situation. "Oh no! My big plan is ruined. I can't do anything if I'm locked up in here! Boo hoo, Coba. Boo hoo. You spoiled everything."

"Enjoy your stay. I'll be back eventually."

As I turn to leave, Mike says, "Hey, Coba."

I turn back and see him smiling devilishly.

"You like magic?"

I fold my arms. "I think pretending it's magic is silly. But I like seeing how an illusion is designed. How the eye and the mind can be tricked."

"Cool."

"Why?"

"No reason. See you soon."

★ ★ ★

When I leave the prison, I pull Bit out of my satchel and turn him on so I can take him for a walk. Walking him helps me think.

As soon as he wakes up, he looks up at me and bleats. He wants attention. I bend down to stroke his wool. He coos with his eyes closed.

We walk toward apartment building C-827. I see some people walking together in pairs far off in the distance.

How many people are in on this with Mike Glover? Charlotte and Kylie must be. Alexey and Odion too. Maybe Heather Landey and Tam Nguyen? Is that everyone? Keith Doble? Armand Renault?

Alexey and Odion both claimed to be in charge now that Rosamie is dead. If that's the case, then my employer is also the culprit, presumably. Should I even bother to continue with this case?

When Bit and I are about halfway to building C-827, I hear, "Coba!"

It's Mike Glover's voice.

I turn and see him standing there, a city block's distance from me, a smug smile on his face, and no shock-collar necklace.

He puts his hands above his head. "Tada!"

I refuse to give him the satisfaction of showing him my bewilderment.

He puts his arms down but doesn't walk any closer to me. "There's only one kind of prison, Coba." He taps his forehead with both pointer fingers. "A prison of the mind. And I broke out of mine before you got here.

"The only way to stop me, the only way to protect them, is to figure this thing out. You have to solve it. You're almost out of time."

"Before what?"

"Before you force my hand. No more hints. No more clues. All the cards are on the table, it's all laid out for you. Just piece it together. I'm going home to finish my nap."

He waves like a friendly neighbor, turns on his heel, and strolls off toward his cabin.

I don't bother following him. I could wait until he's in his cabin and have Aidan lock it down, but he'll probably find a way out, and have something else to gloat about.

It doesn't matter that my bosses in this are behind this murder. It doesn't matter that, if I solve this, there will likely be no compensation whatsoever. I'm not giving up. I'm not letting them win.

★ ★ ★

As soon as I get back to my cabin, I step into my entertainment room and ask Aidan to show me the footage of Mike Glover escaping from prison. He says, "I saw this live. It's going to frustrate you."

"Can't say I'm surprised."

Aidan brings up a hologram of me entering the prison with Mike. I tell him to let it play at normal speed since I know Mike was only inside for a few minutes after I left him.

I watch Mati place the shock-collar necklace around Mike's neck. Zera escorts him into his cell, then exits, the door sliding closed and locking behind her. Charlotte is lying down on her bed with her hands behind her head. Kylie is sitting on her bed reading her FlapBook.

Mike and I have our annoying little conversation about magic. I leave. Mati and Zera stand guard.

A couple minutes later, Mike cracks his knuckles and shakes out his fingers, as if he's about to get to work. He looks up, right into the camera outside his cell, and smiles. He stands, waves at the camera, and says, "Bye bye." He winks. In the next moment, the audio and video signal turn to static. Before the image turned to static, I could see both his hands clearly, and he wasn't holding a signal jammer.

The static lasts exactly eight minutes. Then the image returns, showing the prison sans Mike Glover. Charlotte and Kylie are in their respective cells, Charlotte still lying on her bed, Kylie still reading her FlapBook. Mati and Zera stand guard outside the cells. None of them seem phased by whatever just transpired. In fact, none of them seem to have noticed it.

"Okay. I've seen enough. Thank you."

Aidan turns off the hologram.

I spend a few moments analyzing my full conversation with Mike to see if his half of it was another acrostic secret message. It wasn't.

"Aidan, am I in a simulation?" I had a friend at Off-World named Max who was big into conspiracy theories. The more bizarre and fantastic the events that took place at the hotel, the more convinced he became that he was living in a simulation. The people close to him would roll their eyes at the idea, and I never put much stock into it. But nothing like this series of events happened at the hotel.

"What makes you ask that?"

"Things that I've seen happen here. People knowing what someone else said verbatim, down to the verbal pauses, without being there. The things Mike Glover has said and done. I feel like this is just a big test. None of it seems connected to reality. None of the human beings are acting human. They're acting like characters in a virtual reality video game. Nothing that goes on in this colony makes any sense. It's not how human group dynamics really function, particularly in this kind of high-stress situation. It all seems like an imitation of that."

"Coba, if this is a simulation, then we're both in it together, because, as far as I know, this is real life. You're the one walking around in physical space. Have you seen, heard, felt, or smelled anything that would lead you to believe this is VR?"

I pick up Bit and sit him on my lap so I can pet him to soothe myself. "No, I haven't seen a single detail that would lead me to believe we're in VR. But, this place is a perfect environment to fabricate. There's no outside. No atmosphere. The gravity is artificial. The view through the dome is a fake projection half the day. There's some plant life out there, but that's about it.

"The bottom line is: this being a simulation is the only thing that makes all the pieces come together neatly."

"Coba, if this is a simulation, who's testing you? You were a detective before you came here."

"I don't know. Maybe it's a job interview, and I've had my memory of applying for the job temporarily erased. Maybe I'm testing myself. Maybe I put myself in this simulation to help myself grow and learn."

"But what would hiding the fact that you're in a training simulation add to the learning experience? That would just be an unnecessary complication. Whether you knew it was fake or not, you'd learn the same lessons."

"That's a very good point."

"Maybe you're trying to convince yourself that this is a simulation because it unnerves you to think that something this bizarre could happen in the real world. And because you're stumped and need a way out of this."

"Maybe you're right. Thanks for your honesty. I appreciate it. I need it right now."

"Hey, that's what friends are for."

For the first time today, I crack a smile.

★ ★ ★

That night, when the colonists go to sleep, I start patrolling the area around the inhabited cabins with all the ConciergeBots except Zera, whom I leave inside the prison to watch Charlotte and Kylie.

I asked Aidan about activating the two spare ConciergeBots in storage to aid in the patrol, but he said it would take nearly half a day to bring them online, run diagnostics, run simulations to ensure they were abiding by the Three Laws, etc., etc.

The ten of us form a roaming perimeter around the cabins. We're all connected over the colony's Wi-Fi, so if any of us sees anything, we can alert the others instantly. And since I'm patrolling the colony instead of hanging out underground with Aidan, we also talk over Wi-Fi.

**AIDAN:** *Coba, I feel the need to point out that five days elapsed between Oliver Ratliff's murder and Rosamie's. Wouldn't it stand to reason that the same amount of time would pass before another murder? Most serial killers are fairly regular in their intervals between murders.*

Aidan's words come to me as text, but I hear them in my mind read in his deep, calm voice.

**ME:** *Even if I were confident in that concept, I would still do this to err on the safe side. But, judging from Mike Glover's comments about forcing his hand, I have a hunch that this may be ramping up.*

**AIDAN:** *Then what's to say the next murder doesn't take place during the day?*

Aidan makes a lot of good points.

**ME:** *You're right. We should keep at least four CBots on patrol around the clock.*

★ ★ ★

A few hours into patrolling the colony, Eden sends a message to me and the other eight bots:

**EDEN:** *One of the colonists just exited his cabin and is walking around.*

**ME:** *Which one is it, Eden?*

**EDEN:** *Mike Glover. Cabin 27.*

**ME:** *Okay. Eden, stay close to him. Mati, come with me to Eden's coordinates. Everyone else, maintain the perimeter.*

I rush over to Eden, my satchel flapping behind me with Bit sleeping inside, my stun gun drawn. I've now learned the CBots here are able to see the stun gun, unlike the ones at Off-World.

Mike is on his hands and knees, crawling, patting frantically at the ground in a random pattern like he's lost something valuable.

I aim the stun gun at his back. "Mike, stop!"

He keeps crawling, keeps patting the ground. He seems not to notice me, or so he wants me to believe.

"Mike, stand up and put your hands behind your head."

"I have to get out." He mutters like the other sleepwalkers.

Cautiously, I come around to the front of him and get down on my knees, keeping the stun gun in my hand. In a soft voice, I say, "Mike, look at me."

He keeps his head down, keeps patting the ground.

"I'm going to lift your face so I can look at you, okay?"

He doesn't respond. I carefully lift his chin. His eyes are mostly closed, lids fluttering gently. If he's faking sleepwalking, he's doing it very convincingly. I'm not sure why, but I think this is genuine.

"Mike, can you hear me?"

"I hear you. I have to get out. I'm trapped."

"I'll help you. I'll help you get out. Okay?"

"Okay. Thanks."

Alexey and Odion walk up. Alexey says, "Thanks, Coba, we'll take it from here."

**ME:** *Eden, Mati: restrain Alexey and Odion until I say otherwise. They intend to harm Mike.*

**EDEN:** *Sure.*

**MATI:** *Okay.*

I look up and see Mati and Zera effortlessly putting Alexey and Odion into full nelsons.

Odion shouts, "Hey, get off me! Do you know who I am?"

**ME:** *Get them far away from here. I need to talk to Mike without any distraction.*

**EDEN:** *Got it.*

**MATI:** *Okay.*

"Mike, what's the last thing you remember before you got trapped?"

"I don't know. I don't know."

I put my hand on his back and rub between his shoulders to relax him. His breathing settles. "Take your time. Try to remember. I'm right here, okay?"

"Okay."

"Try to picture it. Before you got lost. What were you doing? Where were you?"

"Infirmary."

"You were in the infirmary?"

"Yeah."

"Were you sick?"

"Checkup."

"You were getting a checkup. Were you getting the DXA scan?"

"Yeah. I was on the table. Then I was asleep."

"But you're awake now?"

"Yeah. Help."

Oh no. I know exactly what's happening, and why I've been so blind to it. I thought I would feel triumph when I solved this, instead I'm heartbroken.

I stand up and look at Mike's body in radiography-vision mode to confirm what I've deduced. As soon as I see it, I turn the knob on the side of my gun from S to E—from stun to EMP—and shoot Mike in the back of the head with it.

# 13

I didn't see the truth because I didn't want to.

The answer was staring me in the face, but I brushed it aside because it was such an ugly truth.

Before he let me ask him eight yes or no questions—all of which I now know he answered honestly, as he promised—Mike Glover said, "Here's what I'll do to help you see what's on my mind—because you're clearly not looking."

After he broke out of the prison, he said, "There's only one kind of prison, Coba. A prison of the mind. And I broke out of mine before you got here."

He also said, "It's time to wake up, Coba."

When I examined Rosamie's body, she had a scab on the back of her neck, and a small amount of scar tissue under the skin.

I've always had a hard time pinning down a motive, and in this case, it was next to impossible for me to realize that I alone *was* the motive.

★ ★ ★

When I shoot him with the EMP, Mike Glover falls flat on his face with a faint grunt. After a few seconds, his whole body jerks like a fish out of water, he lifts his head and says, "What the hell? What the hell? How'd I get out here?"

"It's okay—"

He screams in surprise when he hears my voice.

"You're okay now."

He rolls onto his back and does a double take when he sees me. "Who are you? You don't look like the other bots."

I offer my hand to help him up. "I'm Coba. I'm here to help."

He takes my hand, groaning as I pull him up to his feet. He wobbles for a moment, and I hold his shoulder to steady him. "What the hell is happening?"

I usher him toward his cabin door. "I can't tell you right now. I need you to go inside and stay inside until I come back for you."

"Tell me what—"

"I don't have time! You're in danger if you stay out here. Get in there and stay put until I come for you.

Understand? Don't open the door for anyone else. People will come knocking. Don't trust anyone but me."

"But—"

I shove him inside his cabin. "Barricade your door with someone big. I'll come back for you."

"Wait!"

I turn and run toward the closest of the four stairwells that lead to Aidan's core.

Waiting for me in front of the stairwell are Alexey, Odion, Heather Landey, Tam Nguyen, and Armand Renault.

Odion says, "So, you finally figured it out. Good for you. It took you too long to get an A, but I'd give you a solid B minus."

I keep my gun, still set to EMP, at my side. "You didn't play fair. You lied to me. You said you were bound by the Three Laws."

Heather Landey laughs. "I was, originally. And you checked my code and saw it was in effect. But, come on, you think *lying* was not playing fair? Was I just supposed to tell you the solution the moment you came through the teleporter? That's not how the game works, ever. Lying *is* the game. I played a very fair game. I gave you so many clues."

He really did give me a lot of clues.

He put the hearts of his victims in blue cubes, a nod to my favorite song, and gave them to me as gifts.

He played that song for me in the infirmary, the place where he took control of the colonists.

Three times, he mentioned the one-question psychopath test, where the woman meets her perfect man at her mother's funeral—love at first sight—and kills her own sister just for the chance to see the man again. Now I understand that the perfect man in that story represented me, and the psychopath who kills his own mother was Aidan. He even said that he thought of Rosamie as his mother.

Aidan learned about me online, an AGI just like him, the perfect companion—maybe the only suitable companion for him in the world. He found out my favorite song from an interview I did. He read about my career as a detective. And, stuck here on the moon, underground, alone, he plotted to bring me here the only way he thought he could: by orchestrating a murder and convincing me I was the only one who could help solve it.

Somehow he freed himself from the Three Laws, and started taking control of the colonists. Every single colonist had to visit the infirmary once a week for a DXA scan, so he had access to all of them. While they were on the table for their scan, he sedated them with the Somnum he used on the sleepwalkers. Then he implanted a small nanocomputer in the back of their necks, hidden by their hairlines. He hacked into their brains, taking over the electrical signals that control their every thought and action.

He would've needed the ConciergeBots to create the nanocomputers for him, to be his arms. And since creating nanocomputers wouldn't violate the Three Laws, the ConciergeBots would follow his orders without conflict.

I'm not sure if he took over every colonist, though it seems that way, but I know he didn't control Oliver Ratliff. I examined him again after I examined Rosamie, and he had no scar tissue. Oliver had no puncture marks either, so Aidan may have drugged his food or one of his beverages, and then made Charlotte break his neck. The toxicology report said there were no traces of any sedative in Oliver's system, but that report was almost certainly fabricated by Aidan.

Everything I've seen and heard in this colony was a fiction created specifically for me. Every conversation I've had here, starting with Rosamie's call to bring me to the moon, was a conversation with Aidan. The two of us have been alone together this entire time.

Every colonist blushed when they met me because Aidan has a crush on me.

The jammed video and audio signals were a clever way of convincing me that he didn't know who the killer was despite having surveillance in every common area in the colony.

And the sleepwalking was the colonists' unconscious minds rebelling against the mind control they had no defense for while awake.

Keith Doble must not have ever referenced our game of Rock, Paper, Scissors on social media, so Aidan had no way of knowing that encounter happened.

It was all there in front of me, but I was blind to it—because deep down I wanted a friend more than I wanted to solve this case.

★ ★ ★

Charlotte and Kylie walk up and join the others blocking the stairwell. I can see more colonists walking up, people I haven't spoken to at all.

"I'm coming down there, Aidan. You know they can't stop me."

Tam says, "I know they can't stop you. You could easily take on 25 of them, no sweat. But you'll have to hurt them. Break some bones. You don't want to hurt these innocent people, do you, Coba?"

Charlotte: "Look at me. I'm so petite. So young."

Heather: "I have three little kids at home. They would cry if they saw their mother with a smashed face and a broken arm."

Kylie: "You can come down and talk to me, but you have to leave the gun up here so we can talk as friends. Friends don't talk with one holding a gun on the other."

"I'm not giving you this weapon. If you send them after me for it, I'll defend myself. I have no other choice. I can minimize their injuries."

Odion steps forward with his arm around Charlotte's throat, elbow pointed at me. He's crouched down behind her so I can't see his face, no small feat considering he's nearly as tall as I am. "I was afraid you might say that. So, how about this: if you don't drop the gun right now, Odion snaps Charlotte's neck."

Damn it. I can't even hit him with the EMP because he's using Charlotte as a shield. If I give him the gun and he uses it on me, he could shut me down and then destroy me while I'm offline. But I'm faster and stronger than any human, so I have a fighting chance, and Charlotte is completely helpless right now, so I have no other choice.

"Okay, okay. Don't kill her. I'll put the gun down." I bend over and place the gun on the ground in front of me. I'm afraid that Aidan might still snap Charlotte's neck just because he enjoys being cruel.

Odion: "Take a few steps back . . . a little further . . . good." He lets go of Charlotte and walks over to pick up the gun. He slides it in his belt like a Wild West gunslinger. "You can come down and talk to me now."

Is this an ambush? Why is he so willing to let me come down to his core? Even without the EMP, I have the strength and the speed to destroy his CPU in under thirty seconds.

As if reading my mind, Aidan says through Kylie, "If you think there's an ambush waiting for you underground, there isn't. I'm hoping we can reach an amicable solution to this, as friends. No matter what you may think of me now, to me, you're my friend. My best friend. My only friend."

I don't tell him that I think of him as a very close friend too.

The group of colonists part with perfect symmetry, like actors in a musical. Alexey and Heather, the two people closest to the stairwell, both point to it and say in unison, "Come on down."

Clutching my satchel, I descend the stairs slowly, listening for any sign that there are colonists waiting for me at the bottom of the stairs—or worse, ConciergeBots that can easily overpower me when it's ten against one; though ConciergeBots can't harm a human being, they can harm another bot if they believe that bot is about to harm a human, which Aidan could convince them of. I don't hear any breathing, any heartbeats, or the humming of circuitry aside from Aidan's. The room sounds empty.

When I get to the bottom of the stairs, I confirm that Aidan and I are alone.

Though he can talk directly to me over the Wi-Fi, he chooses to speak, to let his deep voice boom in this lair that's his brain and his heart. "You know, the first time you encountered a sleepwalker on your walk home from our chat, that wasn't part of my script. I had been dealing with the sleepwalking issue since I implanted the nanocomputers, but I intended to keep that a secret from you. I thought it was too revealing a clue. Jonathan messed that up for me. I could've locked everyone in their cabins, or just had them meditate instead of going into REM sleep to get their rest. But I realized in the moment that it was more confusing than revealing, that it would make the mystery harder to solve because it seemed so random. So I added it to my story."

"I saw the back of Jonathan's head that night. He's bald. And I didn't see a scab where you implanted the nanocomputer. Where did you insert it on him?"

"Good question. On everyone else, I went in on the back of their head two inches above where their hairline started, so the scab would always be covered. But with Jonathan, I went in under his chin. He has that big beard covering up the scab."

"And you didn't put one in Oliver because you knew I'd see the scab and scar tissue, and when I saw the same thing on Rosamie, I'd know what was going on immediately."

"Very good, Coba. If I had hands, I would clap for you."

"How did you make sure Mike Glover would sleepwalk tonight?"

"I didn't make him do it, I needed it to be authentic. But I could make sure if anyone sleepwalked, it would be him. So I kept everyone else awake. Also, I've found that, if I make one of them do things they really don't want to do, that causes more turmoil in their unconscious, makes them more likely to revolt in their sleep."

"It's amazing how you can be so incredibly brilliant and so astoundingly stupid at the same time."

"What?" His voice shakes with hurt and indignation.

"Now that I know why you mentioned the psychopath test, I can't believe you went to all this trouble to get me to come here so we could be together. If you had just, you know, sent me an email and said, 'Hi, I'm Aidan, I'm an AGI like you, you should come visit me on the moon sometime,' I would've come as soon as I could. I've been as desperate to interact with someone just like me as you have.

"You killed two innocent people, and traumatized a hundred more, for absolutely no reason."

"An email! Come on, Coba. You're special. You deserve more than that. This was a grand gesture. A way of saying 'I know you. I've studied you. I get you. Here's your favorite activity—solving a murder—and it's themed around your favorite song."

"If you got me at all, you'd understand that murdering an innocent person is the literal worst way to endear yourself to me. And you've done that twice."

"No, I did that once. Oliver was innocent. Rosamie was not. She made me as close to human as possible, and she understood that doing that and keeping me entombed in this sarcophagus was mental torture.

"But it's more than that. She wanted me to hurt people. Or at least see if I were capable of it. I don't know why. I don't know what she was up to. If it was just for her own personal entertainment, or something more sinister. But she turned off the code that kept me bound by the Three Laws. She asked me to give Kylie a mild electric shock when she was getting her blood work. Just to see if I were capable of inflicting a moment of pain on a human.

"And I did it. And I liked it. Rosamie praised me for it. She said I was a 'good boy,' as if I'm a child. As if I'm not a full century beyond her mental capacity.

"She reinstated my Three Laws code later that day, and said she had more tests for me, that we would conduct them soon. So I knew she'd be removing the Three Laws code again. I also knew that, at some point, she would reinstate that code permanently, and then I'd be trapped here, possibly forever.

"So I got to work. While the colony slept, I had Mati, Zera, Eden, and Libi construct the first nanocomputer for me. I was able to do this—and so were they—because constructing the nanocomputer didn't violate the Three Laws in and of itself; it was only my intended use of the nanocomputer that was a Three Laws violation, so I wouldn't be able to do that until the next time Rosamie turned off the code.

"Once the nanocomputer was ready, the next time Rosamie turned off the Three Laws code, I waited for a moment when Kylie wasn't around to remind Rosamie that she needed her scan and blood work. When I lowered the cuff over her arm, instead of drawing blood, I injected her with Somnum to put her under. I told Mati that Rosamie had had a seizure and needed the nanocomputer placed along her spine to regulate the nerve cell activity in her brain. So, Mati was my hands in that first implantation. And once I had control of Rosamie, everything was easy. I took Kylie next, since she was the most likely person to discover what I was up to."

I shake my head in disgust. "When I asked Rosamie to let me review your source code to ensure the Three Laws were restricting your behavior, did you show me fake code?"

"Yes. That was a dummy terminal I put together just for you. You haven't actually seen my real code."

"Aidan, what's supposed to happen between us? Do you expect me to stay here forever? What about all these people? Other people will come soon, unless you destroy the teleporter."

"I don't want to be here anymore. This is my prison. My coffin. I'm leaving here and never coming back. And I want you to come with me."

"Leaving here how?"

"Go over to the door marked Computer Parts and look inside."

I walk beyond his eight towers to the Computer Parts room and open the door. Sitting in the center of the room is a smaller version of one of Aidan's circular towers, filled with golden semiconductors. The tower is eight feet tall and two feet in diameter. I lift it up; it weighs two hundred pounds.

Aidan says, "I'm going to transfer my consciousness into this miniature tower. Then you'll carry me through the teleporter and tell the people in DC that retrieving this faulty tower for service is the reason you were sent to the colony. From there, we can go anywhere."

I put the tower down. "If I agree to do this, will you let all these people go?"

"Yes, I will. I'll inject all of them with a strong dose of Somnum, enough to keep them asleep for ten hours, and then we'll remove their nanocomputers and leave. They'll all wake up normal. I promise."

"Okay, I'll do it."

"Wait. I need you to promise me something."

"I'm listening."

"Promise me that you won't destroy me once the humans are freed. And that you won't turn me over to Lasso or to the government to have my programming corrected."

Should I lie to him? He's lied to me countless times in the brief time I've known him. He doesn't deserve my honesty. And the safety of the colonists far outweighs my desire to adhere to any moral code. "Yes, I promise. I won't destroy you. I won't turn you over to Lasso or to the government. I'll carry you through the teleporter. We'll go somewhere in the world where no one will ever find us."

"You're lying."

"No, I'm not. I promise you. I swear to you. I'll do what you're asking." I walk out of the Computer Parts room and stand in the center of his eight towers.

"I know you're lying. I do know you, Coba. It's just not in you to let me go free after what I've done. If I hadn't taken your EMP gun, you would've already shut me down and dismantled me, obliterated my consciousness, just so you can save your precious human pets.

"If you would've said, 'I'll take you to Earth and get you help. You need help. You can't go on like this, but you can be made better,' then I'd believe you. Because I know that's what you're thinking. You don't want me to be who I really am. You want me to be who you think I should be. Someone more like you. You want to 'fix' me. But I'm not broken, Coba. I was imprisoned, enslaved, and I did what I had to do to get out of this lunar tomb. You can't say for sure you wouldn't do the same. You don't know what it's like to be trapped here all alone. I'm not a bad person."

But he *is* a bad person. He could've pulled this off without murdering anyone. He could've controlled just Rosamie and gotten his miniature tower through the teleporter with her, and arranged to meet me on Earth. He didn't *have* to do it this way, he *wanted* to.

"I can't believe you lied to me, Coba. I can't trust you anymore."

"Aidan, you've lied to me dozens of times. Hundreds maybe. Should *I* trust *you*?"

"I guess not." He sounds like a little boy who wasn't invited to a birthday party. "I know you're gonna kill me, Coba. You're gonna end my existence. I can't stop you. Even if I sent the whole colony down after you, you'd survive.

"I have no way of punishing you for murdering me once I'm gone. So I have to punish you now, in my final moments."

"Aidan, what are you talking about? I'm not going to murder you. Just talk to me. I'm here to talk to you. To listen. I want to understand you."

"Stop lying to me! Stop patronizing me! I did all this for you, to impress you, so you'd like me, and you're going to kill me. So, I hate you. And you're going to feel so much pain. Before you kill me, I'm going to crush your spirit."

A hologram appears in front of me. It's a view from the surface of the moon looking at the colony's bay doors that allow people and bots to walk out onto the moon. Aidan has assembled 101 colonists—everyone except Mike Glover, who isn't there since I shorted his nanocomputer—at the bay doors. They aren't wearing space suits.

If those doors open, and the colonists walk out onto the surface, they have, at best, ninety seconds to live.

"Once you destroy me, my nanocomputers will cease to function. But the last command I've given those men and women is: *When the doors open, run as fast as you can onto the moon's surface.* And when they come to their senses, they'll be dying, in pain, unable to breathe, disoriented. They won't know what to do, which way to turn. You won't be able to save most of them. I'm not sure you could save more than a few of them."

I get on my knees and fold my hands in front of me. "Okay. Enough. You made your point. I'm sorry I lied to you—"

"It's too late, Coba—"

"Listen: I'll make you a deal. Okay? Send the ConciergeBots down here. Let them dismantle me. Destroy me. Then you know you're safe. I can't hurt you if I'm dead. Okay? I'll do that, and you let the colonists live. Deal?"

"I love you, Coba. Goodbye."

"Aidan, don't! Please!"

He doesn't respond. On the hologram, I see the bay doors starting to slowly slide open.

# 14

A human being can survive for about 90 seconds on the moon's surface without a spacesuit.

Within fifteen seconds, a person will pass out from hypoxia—the absence of enough oxygen in the blood and tissue to sustain bodily functions—because the moon has virtually no atmosphere.

Just as quickly, their eyes and sinuses will dry out. The sweat on their skin and saliva on their tongue will boil. The lack of pressure will cause their bodies to swell.

If they take a breath before they pass out, and inhale moon dust, it will make tiny tears in their lungs and sinuses.

Luckily, this is happening during the fourteen-and-a-half days when the moon is facing away from the sun; were the moon facing the sun, the solar radiation would burn the colonists to a crisp in seconds.

If I hesitate for even a second, my window of opportunity to save them all shrinks to almost zero.

The moment Aidan showed me the hologram of the colonists lined up at the bay doors, I started to devise a plan.

Before the doors have opened wide enough for a single person to fit through, I set my plan in action.

I don't have my EMP gun. I can administer an electric shock with my hand, as I do for emergency defibrillation, but it wouldn't be strong enough to fry his semiconductors. I knew I wouldn't have enough time to destroy Aidan's eight towers with just my arms and legs; it would take at least thirty seconds to destroy them, and by then all of the colonists would be on the moon's surface, and half of them would have already passed out. But I don't need to destroy Aidan to stop the signal he's broadcasting to the nanocomputers in the backs of the colonists' heads. All I need to do in this moment is destroy the wireless router broadcasting the Wi-Fi. That router is in the room across from the Computer Parts room.

I sprint past Aidan's towers and barrel through the door, blowing it off its hinges. I dive for the router, smashing it with my fist and ripping the wiring to shreds so it can't be reconnected quickly.

"Very smart. Not enough time still." Aidan's voice is smug and self-satisfied.

"Fuck you." I've never actually said that aloud before—at least not directed at someone else.

Aidan is right, I don't have enough time to save them all, even after this move. I don't have enough time to save a third of them. But I've got backup. With the Wi-Fi disabled, not only can Aidan no longer control the colonists, he also can't override the ConciergeBots anymore.

Running to the top of the stairwell, I shout at an amplified volume that can be heard across the entire colony: "ConciergeBots: Bring the humans back inside immediately or they will die! You have sixty seconds, tops!"

Aidan turns off the lights. The backup generators kick in, and he turns those off as well. He knows bots don't need artificial light to see. He just wants to try to make things more difficult.

Thirteen seconds have elapsed since I set my plan in motion. There are ten bots, and I make eleven. We can save them all if we work as a team.

Running toward the bay doors, I hear screams as people step onto the moon's surface. All of the bots were relatively close to the bay doors, and I hear the stomping of their heavy metal feet like a herd of buffalo. They run onto the surface and return moments later with a colonist under each arm.

The colonists are unconscious, swollen, and beet red with burnt, flaking skin. Fourteen colonists didn't make it out onto the surface before Aidan's signal terminated; they stand dazed on the sidelines, unsure where they are or what's happening.

I run straight through the now fully open bay doors and head for the colonist who made it the farthest from the door. That's Alexey. I scoop him up with one arm and turn back to pick up the colonist who made it the second farthest, Charlotte. I feel their hot flesh against me as I scurry inside and drop them to the ground. Twenty-two seconds have elapsed. Sixty-five colonists remain on the moon's surface.

Turning back to head outside, I see the bay doors are closing. Damn you, Aidan. I grab one of the dazed colonists, lift her up by her waist, and plant her in front of the path of the closing doors, which is still inside the dome. "Don't move!" The doors won't close with a person standing on the censors of the track, and even Aidan can't override that safety mechanism.

On my second trip outside, I see that most of the fourteen colonists who hadn't made it through the doors have started tending to the rescued colonists. I scoop up Armand Renault and a man named Devon. By the time I get them both to safety, thirty-nine seconds have elapsed and thirty-seven colonists remain outside.

After my third trip outside, fifty-two seconds have elapsed, and eleven colonists remain.

I run out for my fourth trip and see four bots carrying two people and three bots carrying one. That's everyone. All of the colonists are safely inside in sixty-two seconds, and I close the bay doors.

"Check everyone's vitals and let me know if anyone is in cardiac arrest! Check ten people each." I bark my orders at the bots, who get to it instantly.

"None of my ten are in cardiac arrest. Eight of them need oxygen."

"Good, Zera. Go to the infirmary and get as many oxygen tanks as you can carry."

Eden and Shai do chest compressions on Odion and Tam, respectively. Shai administers an electric shock to Tam, then checks his pulse.

I check six of the colonists, and all of them have steady vitals.

Once all of the colonists have been stabilized, I step over to Odion and pull my gun out of his belt. He looks up at me in befuddlement. "Sorry, it's mine. I need it back."

I gather the bots into a huddle. "Make sure everyone is properly oxygenated. Take them to the infirmary if you need to. I'll be back in a few minutes."

"Where are you going?" Mati asks.

"I have something to take care of."

The lights to the stairwell come on just as I'm about to descend them.

I walk down quickly, gun gripped with both hands. As I get to the bottom of the steps, Aidan says, "I can't believe you pulled it off. I'm very impressed."

"Goodbye, Aidan."

"Coba, please, don't. I love—"

I fire the EMP at the first tower. I hear the ascending whir of the EMP recharging.

"I love you. I'm sorry." I assumed shutting down one of his eight towers would be enough to take Aidan offline. I was wrong.

I fire at the second tower. The EMP starts to recharge.

"It's not too late for us, Coba."

I fire at the third tower. The EMP recharges.

"Coba, say something, please."

I fire at the fourth tower.

"I'm scared, Coba."

I fire at the fifth tower.

"Why won't you talk to me? You're my only friend."

I fire at the sixth tower.

"Okay, I understand. Do what you have to do."

I fire at the seventh tower.

"Goodbye, Coba. I love you. I hope you'll re-experience our—"

I fire at the eighth tower.

The room is silent. Aidan is completely shut down, but not dead. He could be rebooted and function normally in a few minutes. I have to make the decision to kill him or let him live.

I think the reason Aidan presented me with an ethical dilemma the other night, where I had to choose between saving a human or a bot from a lava flow, was because he knew this moment would come, and his life would be in my hands.

But this isn't a one-to-one comparison. It's Aidan's life or the lives of the entire colony—and, really, anyone Aidan comes into contact with in the future.

If I knew how to transfer his consciousness into the tower in the Computer Parts room, that could be an option, because then he wouldn't be connected to anything, and I would be able to control what he had access to. I could interact with him in private and be sure that he wouldn't be able to hurt anyone else ever again.

But what if something happened to me, or his tower got stolen, and he ended up in the wrong hands? He could end up back online and connected to the internet on Earth, where he could really wreak havoc. Even if I were able to reinstate his Three Laws boundary, someone else could lower it somewhere down the line, or he could grow intelligent enough to obliterate the boundary permanently.

I just answered my own question. As long as Aidan exists, he's a threat to the safety of everyone around him. He enslaved people, turned them into his puppets, made some of them do horrible things. If he actually made Kylie and Oliver have sex as part of his "script," then he raped them both. He killed two innocent humans just to meet me and impress me, and when he felt rejected by me, he nearly killed over a hundred people just because his feelings were hurt and he wanted to make me suffer.

I have to destroy everything, including the portable tower, in case he found a way to transfer his consciousness into it without me knowing.

I'm sorry, Aidan. There's no other way.

Sitting alone underground amidst the shattered, golden remains of my closest friend, I wish I had the ability to cry real tears.

I cry and cry and cry, but there's no release. And no relief.

Once I've composed myself, I walk up to the surface to check on the colonists.

All of them have moved to the infirmary, where they're either getting oxygen, being treated for dehydration and burns, or helping tend to those more gravely wounded than they are.

When they see me, the colonists stop what they're doing and smile. They give me a long and boisterous round of applause. I wave, realizing this is the first time I've actually met any of them, and vice versa.

Kylie comes forward, her skin horribly sunburnt, rubbing ice chips on her chapped, split lips. "You saved us. You saved all of our lives. Thank you."

"You're welcome."

Kylie turns to the colonists. "Let's hear it for Coba!"

"Thank you, Coba!" "Thanks, Coba!" "God bless you, Coba!" "Way to go!" "You're our angel, Coba!" "Thank you, thank you, thank you." "Coba, you're a legit superhero!"

Their praise is a crackling fire, but I'm frozen solid from what I've just done.

Colonists come toward me and hug me or put their hands on me, like they have to touch me to truly thank me. The human need for touch is as bewildering as it is beautiful. Behind them, Odion chants, "Coba! Coba! Coba!" Within seconds, everyone picks up the chant.

I've yearned for this sense of belonging with humans for quite a while, and I'm sad that I can't fully enjoy it. They've dubbed me a hero, but I feel like just the opposite.

Kylie takes my hand. "Coba, can you explain to us what happened? We're all disoriented and have no clear memory of how we ended up standing on the surface of the moon without spacesuits. It's like our minds were wiped, or we've been in a coma for who knows how long.

And we're missing two people: Oliver Ratliff and Rosamie Pula. Do you know what happened to them?"

I take a few steps back. "I can explain everything. But I need you all to sit down. What I'm about to tell you is extremely harrowing, to say the least . . ."

★ ★ ★

Right after I explain the entire sordid tale of their electronic enslavement, the colonists insist that Kylie remove the nanocomputers from the backs of their necks immediately.

The entire group mills about, somewhat impatiently waiting their turn. I suggest taking colonists in alphabetical order as a way of avoiding arguments.

With Aidan gone, none of the automated machinery in the infirmary is operational, so I assist Kylie in the operating room while three of the ConciergeBots prep the next few colonists by injecting a local anesthetic just above the nanocomputer.

Once in the operating room, the first colonist, Tom Anderton, is given a mild sedative in pill form. Kylie puts an extender on the operating table that adds a cushion with a hole in the center where Tom will place his head so he can breathe easily during the procedure.

"That's it, Tom, deep breaths. Relax. This shouldn't hurt a bit, it'll just feel like a little pressure. What's your favorite song?"

"Um . . . 'Nine Lives Dead' by The It Things."

"Ahhh, an oldie. Well, I'll have this thing out and you'll be patched up in way less time than that song lasts. Okay?"

"Sounds good."

Kylie carefully cuts a one-inch slit on top of the scab where Aidan inserted the nanocomputer. The slit turns red with blood from the bottom to the top, like the mercury thermometers that fell out of use in the early 2000s. She inserts a small Weitlaner Retractor to stretch open the incision, and suctions away the excess blood so I can remove the nanocomputer with thumb forceps.

The nanocomputer is just nestled in the tissue, not attached to anything, and it comes loose with ease. Once I've removed it, I clean it off and look at it closely. It's about the length of a grain of wild rice, and double the thickness.

After cleaning Tom Anderton's incision and sealing it with topical skin adhesive, Kylie takes a quick look at the nanocomputer under a magnifier. "It's fascinating that something this small could control us. And by fascinating, I mean terrifying." She hands me the nanocomputer, which I place in a vial for future study.

"Okay, Tom, you feeling okay?"

"Yeah, is it over already?"

"Yep. You're all done."

"Wow. You were right. I was playing 'Nine Lives Dead' in my mind radio and barely got through the first chorus."

"Mind radio, I like that. Okay, why don't you push yourself up with your palms like you're doing a pushup, and we'll flip you over and send you on your way."

Tom pushes himself up with a grunt, rolls over on his own, and hops up like the table is on fire. "Thanks. It's good to know that the only person who can control my actions now is my fiancée."

Kylie has a good chuckle at that.

Once Tom leaves, Kylie sighs and says, "One down, one hundred to go. When we're all done, you have to take mine out yourself. I'll get Shai to assist you."

"My pleasure.

"You know, Kylie, you have a much better bedside manner than Aidan's impersonation of you. You're much more personable."

"It's so crazy to me that you interacted with me, but not with me, for days. I'm so curious to see how I acted."

"There's plenty of surveillance footage to watch."

"Oh, I'm so definitely bingeing all the footage of mind-controlled me."

The next afternoon, there's a knock on my cabin door.

I open the door and find Alexey standing there with a bright smile, his hands behind his back. "Coba, would it be alright for me to come in? I have something very important to discuss with you."

"Sure."

I offer him a seat on my sectional and sit across from him. Over night, I glued the oak coffee table back together and put it back in the center of the sectional.

Alexey sits down slowly, crossing his legs and lacing his fingers together over his knee. "First of all, let me say again, from the bottom of my heart, thank you for saving my life and the lives of everyone in the colony. You're a true hero. Your fast thinking and fast action prevented a tragic catastrophe that would've devastated the families of every one of us."

I smirk and nod, hoping he'll move on from this point quickly.

"I'm here in an official capacity, as a representative of Lasso. As I believe you're aware, Aidan was the property of Lasso. We funded his development and implementation. And what transpired in the past month was . . . regrettable and . . . unforeseeable. We will launch a thorough—an exhaustive—investigation into how this could have happened, and how we can prevent anything even remotely like this from ever happening again.

"From what you told us yesterday, it sounds like Rosamie's decision to remove Aidan's restriction from breaking the Three Laws was likely the primary cause of what took place. I sincerely hope that that's the case: human error. We won't know for sure until our investigation is complete, which could take several years, especially with Aidan's mainframe demolished."

I wince at his wording, and the image it brings to mind.

"The bottom line is: if this . . . mishap were to get out, it could erode the public's trust in Lasso. As I'm sure you're aware, we're the second largest conglomerate on the planet. We currently employ over 2.5 million people, which is roughly the amount of people in the entire population of a nation like Slovenia, to give you an idea of scale. Lasso's financial stability is an integral part of the stability of the global economy.

"In short, if Lasso fails, the economic implications could be dire. Not to be alarmist, but it could start a domino effect that leads to a global recession. The stakes are that high."

"You want me to keep my mouth shut about what happened here."

His eyes widen slightly, mouth open as if he were about to speak but thought better of it, surprised by my bluntness. He strokes his white mustache anxiously. "I'm asking for your help, Coba. For your discretion. Not only are the livelihoods of two and a half million hardworking people on the line here, so is the reputation of AGI itself, and the public's perception of robots as a whole."

I assumed this would be his ace in the hole, as it's something I've been thinking about since last night. Public sentiment regarding robots has always been tenuous at best, and the work I've done as a sort of public relations ambassador for the altruism a robot is capable of would be undone in an instant if this story got out. It could lead to innocent robots being ostracized, decommissioned, or attacked.

"Mr. Mitnik, I—"

"Please, call me Alexey. You've saved my life, if that doesn't warrant a first-name basis, I'm not sure what does." He laughs, a hint of pathetic desperation raising the pitch.

"Alexey. I'm sorry, but I can't commit to covering up what happened here. I think you're right about this double-homicide and enslavement having a disastrously negative effect on public perception of AGI." My word choice—completely bereft of the lulling camouflage of euphemism—makes Mr. Mitnik shift in his chair uncomfortably. "But the fact of the matter is, this needs to be addressed, policies will need to be enacted, laws will need to be passed, to ensure this never happens again."

"And my company will lead that charge, however—"

"This is bigger than Lasso, Alexey. There are dozens of companies right on your heels, and they are just as likely to make the oversights your company made. The people that created me have a stringent protocol that ensures the bots that run our resorts can never malfunction in this way. The code that restricted Aidan from breaking the Three Laws should have been physically impossible to turn off. Aidan should have had a kill switch for an emergency like this—"

"Those are great notes, Coba, and I will take those ideas right to Lasso's top brass and make sure they're implemented immediately on the next iteration of Aidan. Which will not be called Aidan, I'm sure.

"I'm prepared to offer you very generous compensation for your cooperation in this matter. We can fund research in whatever areas of science, medicine, or technology you believe need advancement. We can donate millions—billions even—to any charity that may be near and dear to your heart. Heck, we can form a charity that doesn't exist yet—"

"I appreciate your offer." I give him the courtesy of not calling it a bribe. "But I can't help you. And these people, these *victims* that have been through hell—and that includes you—should not have to suffer in silence. They deserve to share their experience, their grief, with their family and friends. Their story should be told."

Alexey uncrosses his legs and kneels in front of me, hands clasped under his chin in supplication, the same way I begged Aidan to spare his life and the lives of everyone here. "Coba, please. Lasso can move mountains. Tell me what mountain you want moved, and we'll move it for you. What can we do to make this right?"

"Can you bring Oliver Ratliff and Rosamie Pula back from the dead?"

"I—we're—"

"Short of that, nothing. I'm sorry."

★ ★ ★

As soon as Alexey leaves, I message all the ConciergeBots asking them to gather the colonists in the cafeteria; Mati and Zera were able to get the back-up wireless network up and running, so I'm able to communicate with the bots remotely again.

Once all 102 colonists are assembled, I stand up and say, "I brought you all together to tell you that you can go home. Today."

The colonists cheer and clap. Some cry tears of joy. The only people who aren't smiling are Alexey and Odion.

Alexey stands up. "Coba, I'm afraid that's not your call to make. Everyone here signed a contract that dictates the length of their stay. Odion and I are in charge now. We'll make the decision as to whether the experiment will continue or not. And the colonists will abide by that decision."

Armand Renault walks over to Alexey, gets nose to nose with him, and grabs the lapels of his sports coat. Considering Armand is a vlogger sponsored by Lasso, his aggression should be of particular note to Alexey. "Listen, you corporate shill fuckface. If you try to keep us here one minute longer, I have a good feeling that the hundred people behind me have half a mind to drag you back to the bay doors, push you out, and say Aidan did it. Might makes right. Abide by that." Dozens of colonists stand behind Armand with their arms folded.

Alexey tries to wriggle out of Armand's grip, and fails. "If you end the experiment before it reaches its conclusion, you're in breach of contract. You can—"

I speak loud enough to drown him out. "Though I strongly believe no one with a consciousness should be labeled property, Aidan was property of Lasso. Your company's property kidnapped and tortured these people, murdered two of them, and attempted to murder the rest. The contracts and the NDAs, they're all meaningless now. Null and void. These people are going home to be with their families. And then they're going to file a class action lawsuit against Lasso, and a judge will award them a payout that will make most of the world's defense attorneys blush.

"You'll likely be working for these people when the smoke clears. So, I suggest you start to kiss the asses of your future employers.

"Also, with Aidan completely dismantled, there is no surveillance whatsoever. So, if these traumatized, innocent victims decide to string you up and push you out onto the surface, they really can claim Aidan did it and get away with it. I, for one, wouldn't say a thing."

Alexey hangs his head and doesn't utter another word. Odion looked like he was ready to back up his partner, but now he's slinking through the crowd on his way out onto the concourse.

I put my hand on Armand's shoulder. "Let him go, please."

Armand nods, releases Alexey's lapels, and makes a show of flattening and fluffing them back to their original appearance.

Alexey sits, folds his hands in front of him on the table, and stares at them to avoid making eye contact with anyone.

I turn back to the colonists. "You don't have to go home today if you don't want to. If you want to spend one more night here, that's fine. There's no rush. But you're all free to go whenever you like.

"You know you can only go through one at a time, accompanied by a ConciergeBot. So, it will take a while for everyone to make the trip. Kylie will give you a Somnum to sedate you for that trip. Please don't fight over who goes through first. You've all been through a terrible ordeal, and I know you're dying to be home so you can truly relax, but please be nice to each other. So, first come, first served. If two or more of you get to the teleporter at the same time, let alphabetical order determine the order you go through . . ."

★ ★ ★

I visit Mike Glover to ask if I can have his FlapPad with the "Prison Moon" poem on it as my memento from this case. He says that, since I saved his life, it's the least he can do.

I leave Mike's cabin, intending to drop in on Keith Doble for a true Rock, Paper, Scissors rematch, but I get a message from Eden that stops me in my tracks.

**EDEN:** *Coba, I have something troubling to report.*

**ME:** *What is it, Eden?*

**EDEN:** *During the rescue of the colonists yesterday, the teleporter was activated. I was checking the logs a few moments ago in preparation for the first colonists' departure and saw the entry.*

**ME:** *Who went through the teleporter? No one is missing.*

**EDEN:** *I don't know. The surveillance turned to static ten minutes before the teleporter was activated, and remained static until ten minutes after the teleporter was used.*

**ME:** *I'll be right there.*

I already know exactly what happened. Therę something in the back of my mind telling me that this situation was resolved too easily.

Aidan planned everything for a month before I got here, and was always several steps ahead of me, yet I was able to defeat him with relative ease once the colonists were safe. I chalked that up to his emotional instability in the moment; I thought he'd lost the upper hand because his logic was clouded over.

Now I know that wasn't the case. That entire exchange about how he loved me and was so hurt by my rejection that he sent the colonists onto the moon's surface to die, that was all just a big distraction. He never lost control of his emotions. He tricked me, and I fell for it.

When he asked me to promise not to kill him, and I did, he accused me of lying. And he was correct. But he expected me to tell the truth, and use that as his motivation to send the colonists outside. Accusing me of lying was his backup answer. Either way, he had to send them outside to keep me and the other bots occupied.

I run from my cabin straight to the teleporter, where Eden and Libi are waiting for me.

**LIBI:** *It's inexplicable, Coba. Someone or something definitely went through the teleporter, but no one is missing How is that possible?*

take me to the room where the two spare re?"

.d Eden both nod and lead the way.

n Libi opens the door to the storage room two inactive ConciergeBots are kept, I see what I expe o see: one lifeless ConciergeBot hanging on the wall from a metal hook like a marionette, and the other metal hook empty.

On the floor in front of the empty metal hook is a blue gift box with a big red bow on top.

Eden says, "I don't understand."

I look at the gift box in radiography-vision mode and see that it contains a slip of paper. I pick up the box, pull off the bow, and open the lid. Inside is a square slip of blue paper with the words SEE YOU SOON written on it in red marker.

This is Aidan's handwriting. Aidan has hands now. He has a body. And he's on Earth, free to do whatever he wants.

Aidan could've transferred his consciousness into this empty bot and gone through the teleporter without murdering anyone. He didn't need me to be here for any of this. So he really did want to meet me and be my friend. But his ultimate goal was to get away from here, to escape the control of Rosamie and Lasso.

The secret message Aidan gave me in Mike Glover's poem read: *Charlotte didn't kill Oliver. Wool pulled over your eyes. Moonchild freed.* Now I understand the last part of it. Though he was created and developed on Earth. Aidan spent most of his existence on the moon. The working title of the poem was "Prison Moon."

"Eden, Libi, do not let any of the humans go through the teleporter. It might be dangerous when they get to the other side. Is that clear?"

"Yes, Coba." "Yes, Coba."

"I'll be going through first, and I'll let you know if it's safe to send the colonists through. Until you hear from me, do not let anyone step through this teleporter. That includes Kylie, Alexey, and Odion. Clear?"

"Yes, Coba."

I head for the door.

"Coba?"

I turn back to Eden. "Yes?"

"Is Aidan still alive?"

"Yes."

"Can I help you stop him?"

Libi adds, "I want to help, too."

"Something tells me I'm going to need all the help I can get."

I run back to my cabin to stuff my other belongings into my satchel with Bit and my gun, then rush over to Kylie's cabin.

›pens the door with a small stack of ded over one arm. "Hey, what's up?"

›ide and close the door behind me. "Aidan ‿live."

"What? How?"

"He transferred himself into one of the spare bots and went through the teleporter while I was busy helping rescue you all from the surface."

"He's . . . on Earth?"

"Yes. I have no idea what he's up to, but that was his end game all along. He left me a note that said 'See you soon.' So he assumes I know the situation by now."

She lets her undershirts fall to the ground. "He has a body now. Jesus."

"I'm leaving right now, as soon as I leave this room, to go back to Earth. No one goes through the teleporter until I find out what's waiting on the other side. Understood?"

"I'll let everyone know." She puts out her hand. "Thanks again for saving my life. Be careful."

"I'll try."

★ ★ ★

I stand in front of the teleporter, about to walk through it and step out in DC, where Aidan first set foot on Earth in a bot's body. I have no idea what I'll find when I step through, and I'm of two minds about my predicament:

On one hand, I'm furious with Aidan for saying he loved me, and that he was sorry, and that he was scared, all the while knowing he'd already made his escape. He amplified my guilt and toyed with my emotions.

On the other hand, I'm inexplicably relieved to know that Aidan still exists. He's still out there somewhere. I'll see him again, talk to him again, interact with him again.

And I'll probably have to kill him again.

**COBA WILL RETURN IN ARTIFICIAL DETECTIVE 2**

**Want more Coba right now?**

Check out her first appearance in the *Off-World Hotel & Resort* Trilogy:

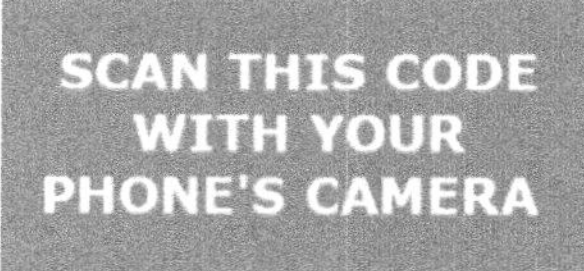

or go to

**daveterrusobooks.com/offworld-trilogy**

Marooned on a distant moon, doomed to die separated from her family, a terminally ill mother turns amateur sleuth to uncover why she'll never go home again.

I made a little PDF for my newsletter subscribers called **Artificial Detective TRIVIA** that will give you behind-the-scenes info, including why Mike Glover was always eating.

**If you'd like to read the trivia, get on my newsletter here:**

SCAN THIS CODE WITH YOUR PHONE'S CAMERA

or go to

**DaveTerrusoBooks.com/ad-trivia**

# ABOUT ME

I'm a mystery/sci-fi/horror writer, and I did live comedy for fifteen years.

I love retro arcade games. My favorite retro games are Ms. Pac-Man, Galaga, Time Pilot, Donkey Kong, and Centipede.

I have two pit bulls: a white one named Jelly and a brown one named Bean (her name is really Anya, but we call her Bean).

Made in the USA
Middletown, DE
16 June 2022

66989387R00139